Unfortunately for Luke, his new and unexpected role as papa had made him desperate.

He needed somebody who knew anything about children—young girl children to be specific.

From what he'd seen so far, Marie fit the bill. Serendipity had brought them together and Luke was determined it would take them a whole heck of a lot farther. He was going to pick her brain until he knew everything she knew about kids. Then he'd walk away. Because getting involved with someone like Marie would be complicated. And he didn't need complicated.

Decision made, Luke picked up his daughter and held her in his arms to keep himself from grabbing Marie and repeating the kiss.

Kissing Marie was dangerous, he'd just discovered. And he was not above using the child to help him keep sight of his goals.

Dear Reader,

March roars in in grand style at Silhouette Romance, as we continue to celebrate twenty years of publishing the best in contemporary category romance fiction. And the new millennium boasts several new miniseries and promotions... such as ROYALLY WED, a three-book spinoff of the cross-line series that concluded last month in Special Edition Arlene James launches the new limited series with A Royal Masquerade, featuring a romance between would-be enemies, in which appearances are definitely deceiving....

Susan Meier's adorable BREWSTER BABY BOOM series concludes this month with Oh, Babies! The last Brewster bachelor had best beware—but the warning may be too late! Karen Rose Smith graces the lineup with the story of a very pregnant single mom who finds Just the Man She Needed in her lonesome cowboy boarder whose plans had never included staying. The delightful Terry Essig will touch your heart and tickle your funny bone with The Baby Magnet, in which a hunky single dad discovers his toddler is more of an attraction than him—till he meets a woman who proves his ultimate distraction.

A confirmed bachelor finds himself the solution to the command: Callie, Get Your Groom as Julianna Morris unveils her new miniseries BRIDAL FEVER! And could love be What the Cowboy Prescribes... in Mary Starleigh's charming debut Romance novel?

Next month features a Joan Hohl/Kasey Michaels duet, and in coming months look for Diana Palmer, and much more. It's an exciting year for Silhouette Books, and we invite you to join the celebration!

Happy Reading!

Mary-Theresa Hussey

Mary-Theresa Hussey
Senior Editor

Please address questions and book requests to:
Silhouette Reader Service
U.S.: 3010 Walden Ave., P.O. Box 1325, Buffalo, NY 14269
Canadian: P.O. Box 609, Fort Erie, Ont. L2A 5X3

THE BABY MAGNET

Terry Essig

Silhouette

R O M A N C E™

Published by Silhouette Books

America's Publisher of Contemporary Romance

For my father,
who actually read encyclopedias
for entertainment.

 SILHOUETTE BOOKS

ISBN 0-373-19435-8

THE BABY MAGNET

Copyright © 2000 by Mary Therese Essig

Visit us at www.romance.net

Printed in U.S.A.

Books by Terry Essig

Silhouette Romance

House Calls #552
The Wedding March #662
Fearless Father #725
Housemates #1015
Hardheaded Woman #1044
Daddy on Board #1114
Mad for the Dad #1198
What the Nursery Needs... #1272
The Baby Magnet #1435

Silhouette Special Edition

Father of the Brood #796

TERRY ESSIG

says that her writing is her escape valve from a life that leaves very little time for recreation or hobbies. With a husband and six children, Terry works on her stories a little at a time, between seeing to her children's piano, sax and trombone lessons, their gymnastics, ice skating and swim team practices, and her own activities of leading a Brownie troop, participating in a car pool and attending organic chemistry classes. Her ideas, she says, come from her imagination and her life—neither one of which is lacking!

IT'S OUR 20ᵗʰ ANNIVERSARY!
We'll be celebrating all year, continuing with these fabulous titles, on sale in March 2000.

Special Edition

 #1309 Dylan and the Baby Doctor
Sherryl Woods

#1310 Found: His Perfect Wife
Marie Ferrarella

 #1311 Cowboy's Caress
Victoria Pade

 #1312 Millionaire's Instant Baby
Allison Leigh

 #1313 The Marriage Promise
Sharon De Vita

#1314 Good Morning, Stranger
Laurie Campbell

Intimate Moments

 #991 Get Lucky
Suzanne Brockmann

 #992 A Ranching Man
Linda Turner

 #993 Just a Wedding Away
Monica McLean

 #994 Accidental Father
Lauren Nichols

#995 Saving Grace
RaeAnne Thayne

#996 The Long Hot Summer
Wendy Rosnau

Romance

 #1432 A Royal Masquerade
Arlene James

#1433 Oh, Babies!
Susan Meier

#1434 Just the Man She Needed
Karen Rose Smith

#1435 The Baby Magnet
Terry Essig

#1436 Callie, Get Your Groom
Julianna Morris

#1437 What the Cowboy Prescribes...
Mary Starleigh

Desire

#1279 A Cowboy's Secret
Anne McAllister

 #1280 The Doctor Wore Spurs
Leanne Banks

#1281 A Whole Lot of Love
Justine Davis

#1282 The Earl Takes a Bride
Kathryn Jensen

 #1283 The Pregnant Virgin
Anne Eames

 #1284 Marriage for Sale
Carol Devine

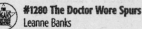

Chapter One

"All right now, let's go through this once verbally before you actually try it."

"Will you quit treating me like a baby?"

"I'm not treating you like a baby. I would never let a baby behind the wheel of a car. Trust me on that. Now backing out of a parking spot can be tricky. If you turn your wheel too soon you can sideswipe the car next to you. You have to back straight out for—"

Rolling his eyes impatiently, Marie Ferguson's nine-years-younger-than-herself but still uncle Jason turned the key in the ignition and ground the engine. "I know how to do this, Marie. I've done it a million times before."

"You've only had your permit for a month and to date have only had a handful of behind-the-wheel opportunities at your driver's ed class. I sincerely doubt you've done this a million— Wait! No! Don't gun it! Look out!" A sickening crunch accompanied Marie's warning. "Oh my God, you didn't check behind you. You hit somebody!"

Jason slammed his hand on the wheel and, in the manner of adolescents around the globe, prepared to defend himself by casting blame on the nearest adult. "It's not my fault. If Dad didn't have such a boat maybe I could maneuver it a little better. I *told* you to talk to him about trading this thing in. It's a dinosaur. An antique. The driver's ed car at school is this cool little—"

Marie sighed and tiredly massaged the ache in her temples with her fingertips. Pain had become her constant companion since taking over Jason's care for her ailing grandfather. "You can harp on Grandpa's choice in automobiles later. Right now we're going to have to get out and exchange insurance information with whomever you just walloped." Marie unlatched her door and struggled out of her safety belt. Then she prayed—out loud so the Almighty would be sure to hear.

"God, please don't let this be somebody with a temper. The day's not even half over and I simply cannot handle any more abuse, verbal or otherwise."

Marie grimaced to herself as she stepped out on the heated blacktop and then concentrated on reversing her frown, doing her best to change it into an apologetic smile which she aimed in the direction of the car behind them. Her smile died before being truly born and Marie cringed at the sight of the ugly dent in the side of Jason's victim's car. The overall visual effect of the scene was greatly worsened by the fact that her grandfather's rear fender was virtually embedded in the other auto's side.

"Lord," she moaned quietly to herself. There was a lot of damage and Marie doubted the recipient of all that damage would be willing to write it off as crash testing. The fact that his car was made of a metal that crushed easily was his problem but Marie didn't think she should even bother bringing that up.

A man climbed out of the injured auto. A very large man, Marie couldn't help but notice. An oversize intimidating male specimen hewn from granite by the looks of him. The sun was still on the ascendant. It had now reached a position directly behind Jason's victim, making it impossible to distinguish facial features. Marie could, however, tell that his hair was both thick and dark. The mirrored aviator sunglasses he wore and his slightly overlong locks were paired with perfectly fitted good quality dress black, or maybe navy—it was hard to tell with the glaring nimbus behind him—pleated slacks, a white shirt that was crisp-looking even in this heat that stretched over yard-wide shoulders, and a red power tie. A modern-day pirate. Oh, God. "Jason," she hissed. "Get out of the car and make nice to the man. Apologize. Grovel. Promise him your firstborn child. Do whatever you have to do to get us out of here alive."

Oh, why couldn't it have been a sweet, understanding, grandmotherly type? Somebody who'd raised children and understood what she was going through. If it had to be a guy, why couldn't it have been somebody wimpy? Anybody other than this body-by-Schwarzenegger type with a face that looked like it would break if he attempted a smile.

Luke Deforest ground his teeth as he reached behind himself with one hand and slapped his car door shut. Damn, but he didn't need this right now. Not that anybody ever needed a car accident, but today, when his temper was greased and he was running tight on time... Well, now was not a good choice.

Luke slammed his hood with his fist in frustration and turned away from the apprehensive duo approaching him. Get a grip, he advised himself. Accidents will happen. The kid hadn't intentionally picked the worst day of Luke's life to back into his three-month-old-interior-still-smelling-like-new-candy-apple-red car of his dreams—the little donkey's heinie.

Luke's knuckles whitened as he continued to list like a litany all the reasons he shouldn't knock the little jerk's head right into the middle of next week. But damn, he needed to make a good impression today. An awful thought struck and Luke ruthlessly pushed it back. Certainly the car was still driveable. Of course it was. Luke glanced down the side of his car. No, it wasn't.

Luke took a deep breath, turned back to face the duo and pinned the driver of the offending vehicle with his gaze. Even through the glare of today's strong sun, he looked young, Luke thought and was immediately appalled. When had teenagers started looking like such babies, he mused. Was it a sign of his own creeping dotage that had him wondering when they'd started allowing ten-year-olds to start driving?

Nah, he was only thirty-four. It wasn't Luke getting old, it was just this child dressed in adolescent's clothing pretending to be sixteen. No way. Luke directed himself to the woman who'd climbed out of the passenger's side. He hadn't gotten a good look at her yet, but she at least appeared to be of legal age. On the short side of average, she was slender and trim. Her hair glinted red in the sunlight, her skin was pale, and even from this distance he could see her eyes were blue. In fact, she bore a striking resemblance to his brother's wife. He squinted and did a double take. Good God Almighty, it was Marie. Wasn't it?

"Marie?" he checked.

Marie did her own double take. No. It couldn't be. Then she sighed philosophically. Well, her life had certainly been going to hell in a handbasket of late. This would certainly be right in keeping. Somehow Jason had managed to ram her grandfather's car right into her ex-brother-in-law. Wonderful. Wade's brother had seemed to almost purposely avoid them after their wedding. She doubted he'd be any too happy to see her now.

"Luke?"

"Yeah. It's me."

"What are you doing here? I thought you lived up in Michigan somewhere." And if he'd only stayed there Jason wouldn't have hit him. Jason was right, the accident wasn't his fault. It was Luke's. Luke didn't belong here in Elkhart,

Indiana. He belonged far, far away. The farther the better. She didn't need any further reminders of her previous life, especially not Wade's incredibly handsome big brother who'd always made her feel like an adolescent with a crush. Thank God no one knew about that. She'd never breathed a word to a soul. She'd met Wade first and fair was fair.

Luke nodded his head toward Jason. "He old enough to be behind the wheel?" he asked. "I'm going to be mighty upset if you're letting him drive around without any insurance coverage," he warned.

Marie swallowed hard. If he was trying to be intimidating, it was working. She definitely felt threatened. She hastened to reassure him. "Oh, yes, he's old enough," Marie said. "Fifteen and a half, as a matter of fact. Jason has a learner's permit rather than an actual license, but he's permitted to drive so long as there's a licensed driver in the car with him."

Jason, obviously insulted at this slur to his character, had already produced his permit. He reverently unfolded it and smoothed out the crease before presenting it for inspection.

"Hmm." Luke studied it and all but grunted. "You've got insurance?" He pinned Jason with a laser stare.

"Sure I do," Jason retorted, then turned to Marie questioningly. "Don't I?"

"Absolutely," she assured him with a nod of her head. "I took care of that before I even took you over to the Bureau of Motor Vehicles to get your permit." She took a deep breath and approached Luke. "We're definitely covered." She extended her hand. After a brief pause, Luke took it. "How's it going, Luke? It's been a while." Since your brother's funeral to be exact, she silently added.

Luke's handshake was quick and cursory, the amenities covered then forgotten. Good thing she hadn't attempted a hug or anything else that would have really invaded his personal space. How could she have ever wanted this man?

"You remember my, uh, uncle, Jason Fort. You met briefly at the wedding and again at the, um, funeral."

Luke reluctantly nodded his head. "Jason," he acknowledged. "First time I haven't seen you all slicked up. Didn't recognize you for a minute there." Luke turned his head to glance significantly down the length of his car. "We've got ourselves a little problem here, Jason, old buddy," he said as he viewed the wound in his red compact.

Jason nodded glumly. "Yes, sir."

Luke and Jason stood there with their hands in their front pockets studying the damage with grim looks. They studied it so long, in fact, that she began to worry. Men, she'd noticed from her own relationships, tended to take damage to their automobiles as a personal affront. You'd think he'd be grateful nobody was hurt, Marie thought waspishly. But no, the way he was staring at his car's backside, you'd think he felt its pain. "It's not terminal, or anything," she said. "I mean, it can be fixed. Right?" she asked a bit helplessly as she gestured to the ugly gash.

Luke grunted.

Marie took that for affirmation.

Luke never took his eyes off his scarred but still proud automobile. Finally, he drawled, "I suppose it's fixable. It's just not driveable in the here and now."

"What's that mean?" Marie asked suspiciously.

"It means I've got an appointment in Kalamazoo in a little over an hour."

Marie looked at her own watch as if to verify his appointment. "You're not going to make it."

"I know. Especially if we don't get a move on here. Well, I hope you and Jason don't have plans for the rest of the afternoon. If you do, you'll have to cancel them. I must have something in the trunk Jason and I can use to pull the metal away from the wheel. I'll leave my car in the lot here. There's no time to mess with it now. I'll have to deal with it when we get back."

Marie stared at her former brother-in-law in dismay. "What are you talking about, *we?* I'm not going anywhere except home to some extra-strength pain reliever and a darkened room."

"That's what you think. You wanted a nap, you shouldn't have let Crash here behind the wheel of a car."

"I didn't know I was going to need to lie down until five minutes ago," Marie muttered through clenched teeth. Men. She was surrounded by them and they were all bent on driving her insane. As soon as her grandfather was home from the hospital and operating without a walker she was joining a convent. For real this time.

Luke shrugged and glanced at his watch. Damn, it would have to be Marie. She was a hell of a looker and Luke had noticed. Man, had he noticed. It was one of the only times in his life he could remember being jealous of a brother whose life, in Luke's estimation, had been pitiable. A shallow man interested only in the surface. It angered Luke that he himself found Marie's surface interesting when she was very likely every bit as shallow as his brother. She'd married him, hadn't she? Luke had stayed away as much as possible, disgusted with himself and the situation. Women watched soap operas with plots like this. He certainly wasn't going to star in one. But today he had no choice.

"There's a drugstore in the mall. Run in and buy yourself whatever you need for your headache. We've got a little under five minutes before I absolutely have to be on the road. Buy enough for two. Better make it extra-strength whatever it is. I seem to be developing a major migraine myself in the last few minutes."

And men complained women were illogical. She'd like to see a researcher try to flow chart a man's thought processes some time and see how far they got. "Luke, what are you talking about? I mean, I'm sorry if you have a headache and certainly I'll be contacting our insurance company and we'll take care of any damages but—"

"You're down to three minutes," Luke interrupted, checking his watch once more. "Then we're leaving for Kalamazoo. And by the way, I'll be doing the driving."

"Kalamazoo!" Marie yelped. "I can't—"

"Come on, Crash, give me a hand here. I think I've got a tool kit back in the trunk." Luke popped his trunk and seemed surprised to see Marie still standing there when he glanced up. "Move, woman! My headache and my incapacitated automobile are both courtesy of you and your uncle. The least you can do is help me keep my appointment."

Marie closed her eyes in defeat. Forget it. She'd never win. Her headache had reached such proportions she doubted anything would help. "Never mind," she sighed but she doubted they heard, so engrossed was the twosome in debating the merit of one tool after another for its metal-bending properties. Marie trudged her way back to the driver's side of her grandfather's car's. Climbing in, she turned the key in the ignition and gently, carefully pulled slowly forward, disengaging her grandfather's bumper from her dead ex-husband's brother's car. Marie shook her head. Her life had hit an all-time low with this one. Surely things would improve from this point on. After all, they could hardly get worse. Could they?

They could.

And did.

Marie rested her head on the steering wheel while she waited. Evidently she was on her way to Kalamazoo. Brief moments later Luke opened the door behind her and threw a shopping bag into the rear seat. Jason slid in beside it. Luke then opened the driver's door. "Move over," he directed.

Marie thought about arguing, decided it wasn't worth it. "Fine," she muttered as she scooted over. "Let the macho man drive. God knows a mere woman can't be trusted behind the wheel of a car."

Luke wasn't feeling overly charitable when he switched on the engine. "Glad you realize it. Saves time. Now, fasten your safety belt."

"Yes, sir," Marie grumbled. Even a poor pitiful specimen such as herself knew enough to strap in, for heaven's sake. Especially when a close relative of the original kamikaze pilot was steering. Ah well, she was numb anyway. She probably wouldn't even notice all the close calls. Provided they remained close calls.

"You can just drop me off on your way out of town," Jason called from the back seat.

Like hell, Marie thought. Why should she be the only one to suffer?

"No time," Luke said, denying the request before Marie could open her mouth. "It's going to be close as it is."

He had them out of the lot and headed toward Kalamazoo and away from home base before Jason could do more than sputter.

Marie couldn't help but admire his style. And Luke was a surprisingly good driver. His brother, Marie's ex, had driven like a maniac. Live by the sword, die by the sword, Marie thought once more. She was only grateful Wade had been alone the day he'd finally done himself in. Marie gradually relaxed as Luke competently handled the wheel. She rode in silence, head back, eyes closed, letting her headache ease as the car smoothly ate up the miles.

"Idiot," Luke muttered as he was cut off. He braked sharply and the shopping bag he'd tossed onto the back seat tipped over.

Jason righted the bag and began stuffing the spilled contents back in. "Little old for stuffed animals, aren't you?" he asked as he retrieved a plush teddy bear from the floorboard and tossed it back into the bag.

"Why'd you cut things so close if all you needed was a baby gift?" Marie asked irritated all over again that he'd been where he shouldn't have been, thus causing the accident.

"It's for the meeting," Luke muttered while he checked his mirror, signaled and zipped around a slow-moving truck.

"What kind of meeting requires teddy bears?" She turned around in time to see Jason pick up a thermal-weave blanket with satin binding and bound into a neat bundle with paper tape and plastic wrap. "And baby blankets?" she inquired suspiciously. "What, you're on the board of the Kalamazoo orphanage?" Somehow the image just didn't fit with his current piratical, swashbuckling look and her former impression of him.

"I'm picking up my, uh, daughter," Luke admitted grudgingly, his cheeks stained red for no reason Marie could think of. "I have to meet with some social workers first."

Marie's brows rose and her eyes widened as she considered that tidbit. Well, there was certainly little that could be said. First of all, she hadn't even known he *had* a daughter. For sure Wade had never mentioned it and she'd never seen hide nor hair of a child in any of her previous encounters with Luke.

"How old is your daughter?" Marie inquired before caution got the better of her.

"Two. I think."

He thought? He didn't know his own child's age? Marie sat back in her seat. Well, she'd figured out the Deforest family was seriously messed up about a month after her wedding. She supposed she shouldn't be surprised that Wade's older brother had to have his toddler released to him by a social worker. And she wasn't exactly in a position to throw stones, was she? Her only family seemed to be specializing in the bizarre and unusual themselves, what with her taking on the task of raising her own uncle. Well, it was certainly nothing to her, Marie decided. She'd simply make sure she was out of the picture by the end of the afternoon. Luke could have the social worker come and live with him for all she cared. Marie just felt sorry for the poor, obviously neglected child.

"What's her name?" she couldn't help but ask.

"Carolyn."

"Pretty."

"It's okay, I suppose."

"You don't like it?"

"Not particularly."

"Then why'd you pick it?" Marie's headache was beginning to flare up again.

"I didn't. Her mother did. I had no say."

The mind boggled. What was the mother, a female sumo wrestler? Marie couldn't begin to imagine a circumstance, any circumstance where Luke Deforest wouldn't have a say—wouldn't make darn sure he had a say.

Marie decided not to pursue it, however. The answer was bound to only further confuse her. The entire day had taken on a surreal quality. Nothing was making sense. She'd read stories where people walked through mirrors or wardrobes and found themselves trapped in an alternate world. Under the circumstances, the best thing to do was go through the motions and pray for the sun to set. Maybe by the time it got around to rising again she'd wake up on the right side of the mirror.

One could always hope.

Unfortunately, more often than not of late, she'd found herself spending time on the backside of the mirror.

Actually, she was developing a certain bizarre fascination with life on the wrong side. One never knew what would pop up next. Rabbits with pocket watches, incredibly arrogant and macho—not that Marie was into macho, because she most certainly wasn't—pirates in red sports cars. Who could predict?

"What do Jason and I do while you're at this meeting?"

"I don't know. Read a book or something."

"What book? You hijacked us from the mall parking lot, remember?"

"Okay, so take a walk."

"Is the area safe where we're going?"

"I've never been there before."

Marie threw up her hands. "Fine. Great. I'm taking a nap now. Wake me when the nightmare's over. Good night." And she leaned back, folded her arms across her chest and closed her eyes.

In the rear seat, Jason apologetically cleared his throat. "Ahem. Marie's a little high-strung. You have to learn to just kind of ignore her like I do."

Marie didn't open her eyes, but she snorted her opinion of that.

Luke wove his way through a knot of cars. "Maybe you ought to listen a little harder, at least when she's giving driving instructions."

Amen to that, thought Marie and crossed her arms the other way.

Luke glanced at the boy in the rearview mirror. "And as for my learning to tune her out, we don't see enough of each other to make it worth worrying over."

Amen to that, too. And let it stay that way.

Marie actually fell asleep. When she startled awake, the car was parked on a shady street with the windows all left open a few inches for air circulation. She rubbed her eyes, sat up and looked around. Where was she?

Turning around to glance down the block, she found Jason in the back seat with earphones plastered on his head and his portable CD player making him deaf. He wiggled his fingers at her in a gesture of recognition as his head bobbed rhythmically. "Where's Luke?" she mouthed and Jason pointed to the building across the street.

Marie briefly studied the building, but it wasn't giving

away any secrets so she turned her attention back to Jason. "You're going to lose your hearing, you know," she said.

Jason pointed to his ears and shrugged, indicating he couldn't hear her over the noise being pumped in.

Marie sighed and turned around. At least he wasn't sharing his musical choice with her. She should be grateful for small favors.

Marie tipped her head one way and then the other. She glanced at her watch. Good grief. She'd been asleep for almost forty-five minutes. No wonder she had a crick in her neck. To tell the truth, she was a little worried with the way she fell asleep at the drop of a hat lately. Her periods were off, too. It had to be the stress. Please, God, let it be stress.

Unfastening her belt, she opened the door and stepped out onto the sidewalk. She needed to stretch out. At the end of the block she turned around and marched back up the street. By her fourth passby she'd developed a 'glow'— her mother had always insisted ladies didn't sweat—and all the kinks were well worked out of her legs. She strode quickly by Jason's lanky reclining-yet-still-rhythmically-twitching form when suddenly her quiet humming was drowned out by ungodly screeching.

Startled, she swiveled about. Half a legion—at least—of women were being raped or abducted somewhere, but where?

She searched the area, and what to her wondering eyes should appear but Luke, coming down the steps of the building Jason had pointed out earlier. He held a toddler in his arms, but rather than cradling her up against his body, he held the little one out and away from himself, as though he wanted to distance himself from his own daughter, the source of all that noise. And he had an exceedingly pained expression on his face.

"Curiouser and curiouser," Marie murmured and crossed the street to him.

"Hey, hey," she said and rubbed the child's back soothingly. At the same time she pushed the child up and against Luke's chest. The pained look on his face became even more pronounced.

"It's all right, sweetheart," Marie crooned. "Daddy's got you. Everything's okay. Daddy will fix everything, won't you, Daddy?" When Luke didn't speak up quickly enough to suit her, Marie poked Luke in the ribs as a prompt to answer. It was her feeling Daddy shouldn't have to think quite so hard before responding.

"Ouch! What'd you do that for?" He glared at her. Damned woman had been a pain since the moment he'd run—scratch that—*she'd* run into him.

Marie glared right back and gestured to the sobbing toddler. The noise level had dropped but people were still staring and they were still only a few decibels below eardrum shattering.

"Oh, right." Luke cleared his throat. "Marie's right, Carolyn. Dad's got the situation under control." He wished. "You can stop screaming. It's not going to change anything, after all and if you'll just stop and think for a minute I'm sure you'll realize—"

Marie reached up and snatched the baby right out of his arms and hugged her to her breast. "Oh, for God's sake. Come here, sweetie. Let Auntie Marie hold you." Marie wrapped her arms snuggly around the baby so she'd feel secure, rested her cheek on the top of little one's head and began to rock in place. "Shh, shh, Auntie Marie's got you now and she won't let anything happen to you."

Luke rolled his eyes and muttered, "Oh, brother."

Marie sent him an evil look and mouthed, "Go get the blanket you bought."

"What? I can't hear you. Carolyn, you've simply got to pipe down before you permanently damage our hearing. Now, what did you say?"

Marie refrained from kicking him in the shins. Barely.

Very softly she instructed, "Go and get the baby blanket you bought."

"You're still mumbling," Luke complained. "Did you say you wanted the pink blanket? What for? Marie, look at her. She's all red and overheated. The last thing she needs is a blanket. She must be getting heavy. Let me take her back."

She finally blew up. "So you can make her cry again? The blanket's a comfort thing, you dolt! You probably had one yourself at her age. Or maybe you didn't and that's what's wrong with you. Now would you just quit arguing and go get it?"

Luke backed away and made a calming gesture. "All right, okay, I'm going, see? But I'd just like to point out I'm not the one who made her cry again. If you were all that good with kids you'd know not to yell like that. It upsets them."

Marie ground her teeth. For two cents she'd hand the child off to him and sit back to watch the show. Unfortunately they'd all be sharing the same car for the next hour and the screaming was already grating on her nerves. "There, there, sweetheart, I'm sorry. It's just that men are such morons, sometimes your only option is to cut loose." Marie continued to rub Carolyn's back while she vilified all men in a soft croon. "You'll see. Someday you'll come to me and say, 'Auntie Marie, I remember back when I was no more than two and you told me all about men. You were right, Auntie Marie. They are dolts.' Now let's go down to the car, all right, honey? I'll introduce you to another of the species. *Homo Sapiens Adolescenti,* an absolutely pitiable group. The worst of the worst. You remember that when you're sixteen and don't have anything to do with them, okay, sweetheart? Save yourself all kinds of grief."

By then they'd reached the car. Luke had finished unwrapping the blanket. He held it out to her.

"Just drape it over her," Marie directed. "Make sure the satin touches her cheek."

"Right. But I still say she's going to suffocate." Luke carefully covered his daughter, arranging the folds just so. "How's that?"

Carolyn snuffled twice then turned off the spigot altogether.

Marie sighed. "Wonderful. In another hour or two the birds may even feel safe enough to begin chirping again."

Luke reluctantly grinned. "Yeah. It was pretty scary, wasn't it? I've got to run back in and get her car seat. I'll be right back."

"Coward," Marie said, but she smiled and snuggled Carolyn while they waited.

Carolyn had so exhausted herself with all the carrying on, that she conked right out within minutes of the car being in motion. Blessedly, she slept the entire trip through.

"Well, that's done," Luke said as he pulled into his own driveway. "I think I've got enough time to make arrangements to get my car towed in and get a loaner. Tomorrow you can take me over to pick up a rental."

Marie sighed. She supposed it would be mean-spirited to say no. The accident had been their fault, after all. "Sure. I guess."

"Call your insurance agent when you get home. We'll exchange insurance information and stop by the police station when I see you tomorrow."

"Yeah. Right." Man, she really didn't want to do this. Besides having the personality of a prickly pear, Luke was a reminder of a painful period in her life. "Twelve o'clock?"

"Sounds good. See you then."

"Right." Marie put the car into Drive while she waited for Jason to get back to the car after helping Luke in with Carolyn's stuff. She wanted out of there just as quickly as possible. She had a feeling that the longer she stuck around Luke Deforest, the worse off she'd be. And the effect he seemed to have on her was only the half of it. Luke Deforest was trouble with a capital *T*.

Chapter Two

Instead of sliding into the passenger side, Jason came
around to the driver's side. Marie sighed. She should have
known.

"Scoot over, Marie. I'll drive now."

Only over her dead body. "Sorry, Jason, but I'm driving.
One accident per day is about all I can handle."

Jason rolled his eyes. "Oh, come on. You can't be serious."

But Marie stood firm. She'd reached her quota of ado-
lescent-style thrills and chills for the moment. It was either
stand firm or flip out. Marie knew which one she preferred.
"No. I'm afraid there's no negotiating this one." Ha, there
was a misnomer if ever there was one. More like gross
intimidation wouldn't get the adolescent his way this time.
Unfortunately for Jason she was too numb to be properly
cowed by the prospect of one of his scenes. "I'm driving,"
she assured him firmly. "Jump in and let's go before Luke
comes out to see what's wrong."

That threat worked. Luke was twice his size and not
happy with the accident. Jason knew he'd gotten off easily.

He still had all his appendages, was still breathing, wasn't he? He moved. Not particularly graciously, but he moved.

He also scowled. He stomped around the front of the car, slapping the hood with his fist as he circled in front of it. He slammed the door when he got in and immediately began complaining. "Man, one little mistake and everybody's all over you. Like I already told you, this wasn't my fault. If Dad would just buy me a decent car none of this would have happened. He can keep this boat for all I care, but you could talk him into getting me something cool. I know you could."

Marie rolled her eyes in resignation. Jason was on a roll. She was in for a good half-hour sermon on why Jason needed a new car, preferably a sports model with a trunk big enough for a mega stereo system complete with something called a subwoofer. Marie had asked around. It seemed that this subwoofer thing was for the hormonally impaired. It magnified bass sounds. It was what made your car shake when you were stuck at a red light next to some testosterone-challenged adolescent whose entire vehicle shuddered on oversize tires while emitting low *boom boom de boom* sounds. Allowing that thing into her house or car would be tantamount to dying and going to hell. She'd be permanently stuck at a red light that would never turn green, at least not for her.

No way. Not a chance.

Marie had never had an inclination to indulge in alcohol before but she was seriously thinking about taking up drinking. If she was declared unfit wouldn't somebody else have to take over the job of seeing Jason through until her grandfather was back on his feet? Didn't the Red Cross deal with disasters? Surely Jason qualified. There had to be somebody. Anybody.

When Jason showed no signs of letting up, Marie decided to break into his diatribe. "Even though the accident was clearly Luke's fault for having the poor judgment to be behind you when you decided to back up, it's your insurance premiums that will go up," she informed him grimly as she gently eased the car into traffic. "You're going to have to study a bit harder next semester. A 3.0 gpa will get you a good student rate and help counteract what just happened."

Jason only shrugged. "The light's changing. Better slow down."

The attitude and running commentary on her driving put her back up. She'd rather deal with Luke Deforest— Why did her thoughts keep coming back to Luke? He wasn't as blatantly handsome as Wade had been. No, his attraction was more insidious. It sneaked up and got you on a subconscious level. Rotten male. Marie tapped the brakes. "I know what color the light is and I'm serious here. For your information, teenage boys and girls in their early twenties have the highest rates. You can't afford to make it any worse by messing around with your grades."

"No skin off my nose," Jason informed her. "Dad's going to have to pay whatever it costs anyway. I sure don't have the dough. That pittance of an allowance you talked him into doling out doesn't cover more than a pack of chewing gum. You really fell down on the job there, Marie."

Marie snorted as the light she'd stopped for changed and she again accelerated. "You buy mighty expensive chewing gum is all I can say. Like twenty dollars a pack. And maybe I could have talked him into more but I didn't and I won't. Twenty dollars is plenty for somebody your age." She almost had to bite her tongue to prevent herself from telling him about how little she'd gotten when *she'd* been his age. It would make her sound too old. Too much like the parents who lectured their ungrateful kid about how *they'd* walked four miles each way barefoot through the snow to get to school, uphill both directions and furthermore, they'd liked it. Marie refused to permit herself to fall onto the wrong side of that generation line. She'd much rather be on the eye-rolling side even though the temptation was severe and she faithfully checked her hair every morning ever since her grandfather had shattered his hip to make sure none of the strands had grayed overnight.

But Jason wasn't done yet. "You just don't get it. I mean, were you *ever* young? It's like totally demeaning to have to ask my niece for money, you know. None of the other guys have to do anything so lame. Their parents don't give them stupid curfews of eleven o'clock on the weekend. They can stay out as late as they want and they all get however much money they want."

"Yeah, right. Sure they do." Marie turned a corner. She felt oddly bereft as she lost sight of the street Luke lived on. "Give it up," she advised. "It's not going to happen. The plan is, I'm going to discuss this with Grandpa and I'll advise him to pay the equivalent of the cheapest insurance rates. I think he'll listen, too. That means you'll have to fork over the difference between that and whatever the actual charge is."

"I don't have any money," Jason repeated slowly as though Marie were mentally slow and couldn't grasp simple concepts. "No moola, get it? Zero *dinero*. Zip."

Marie turned off onto another side street. They were almost home. Thank God. Maybe she could escape up to her room for an hour or two. "Guess you'll have to get a job, huh, Jase?"

"I'm not sixteen yet," Jason informed her smugly. "No one will hire me."

Marie patted his arm bracingly. "Sure they will, kid. Ever hear of a work permit? If twenty dollars a week really isn't enough to keep you in the style you're accustomed to or you need extra cash 'cause you don't qualify for the good student discount, why, I'll be happy to get Grandpa to sign for one. No problem."

"Think you're so smart," Jason muttered under his breath and braced himself. "Watch the kid on the bike."

"I see him, I see him."

"The speed limit's twenty-five. You're doing almost thirty. How come your hands are on ten and two? My driving instructor says they should be on nine and three so the airbag doesn't break them if it goes off. Of course he's only a total loser. His airbag probably goes off every day of the week and twice on Sundays."

"Jason, I've been driving for eight years now. I think I can handle it."

"Couldn't prove it by me," her uncle said under his breath. "There's a car coming. Watch him."

"I'm watching him, Jason, I'm watching." Marie wondered how parents ever put up with getting their kids through to their licenses. Especially if they had more than one. If Jason corrected her driving one more time, she'd be forced to murder him. There wasn't a judge in the country that would convict her, either. Not if they'd had any kids with learner's permits of their own.

Marie knew better than to get drawn in. She absolutely did. She should just ignore him. That would be best. Ignoring Jason, however, was a bit like trying to ignore a nest of disturbed wasps. It was damned hard not to notice all the little pricks and harder still to keep from swatting back.

"Stop sign at the end of the block."

Marie's knuckles were white against the steering wheel when she blew. "Shut up, Jase," she directed. "Just...shut the heck up."

The car safely garaged once more, Marie called her insurance company, then retreated upstairs. She pulled the shades down and hid in her bedroom for an hour. Teaching Jason how to drive was going to make an old woman out of her in next to no time. She had to fight the urge to get up and go check her hair in the mirror.

Luke Deforest probably found gray hair a turn off.

What? How stupid. She didn't—shouldn't—care what Luke Deforest thought about her hair or any other of her body parts. Yes, she did. Well, she'd get over it. She'd see to it.

Marie took a deep breath and held it, then slowly exhaled. This was all Jason's fault. He was making her lose her mind. After all, what did she know about dealing with an adolescent? Heck, she'd been one herself not that long ago. Finding herself so quickly and abruptly on the receiving end of all that adolescent garbage was throwing her psyche into shock, that was all.

Marie took another deep breath, slowly exhaled and dug out an old Paul Simon CD, curled up in her favorite reading chair over in the corner and vegged out while Paul crooned softly in the background. Of course she was damn lucky to hear him at all over the *boom de booms* emanating from just down the hall. Still, it was soothing. When Marie finally emerged, she went down to the kitchen confident she was once more in complete control. For sure she wasn't going to give Luke Deforest another thought. Maybe she should bake some cookies and take them with her to their meeting tomorrow. See if she couldn't soothe the savage beast. She could always say they were for Carolyn so he wouldn't suspect anything.

Marie produced a small meat loaf for dinner which precipitated a lot of gagging sounds and threats to hurl up the meal, but honest to God, you couldn't serve pizza every night, could you? Pepperoni was not exactly the best example of the protein group you could find. The salad was put away untouched except for the small portion Marie herself had taken.

Marie was pathetically grateful when, after downing half a container of double fudge brownie ice cream, Jason cleared out of the kitchen without offering to help or doing so much as clearing a dish. Frankly, she'd rather do it herself than have to put up with her uncle for ten more seconds. The sound of his bedroom door shutting—loudly—came as a blessed relief. And then the house began to shake. *Boom boom de boom.*

No way was she getting that subwoofer thing for him. Absolutely not. Why would any sane person pay money to make a bad situation degenerate to worse? She turned an oldies station on the radio all the way up to camouflage Jason's exaggerated bass and sang along with Aretha Franklin, shaking her hips while she finished cleaning the kitchen. R-E-S-P-E-C-T. Oh yeah, her and Aretha, they were both craving it, needing it.

Lord, she was obviously overtired. She was going to bed.

Shortly before noon the next day, Marie rang Luke's doorbell. She'd spent time choosing her outfit, applying her makeup and had actually plugged in the curling iron and worked on her hair. She waited for Luke to answer, pleased that she could still pull herself together into a decent package. It had been months since she'd bothered to try. She'd settled for clean ever since assuming responsibility for Jason. Who was there to impress? One of his acne-riddled, fifteen-year-old buddies? No, thank you.

Luke, on the other hand, was fair game. He'd intimidated her the day before, looking better than any man had a right to, almost like some kind of male model for crying out loud. Except there'd been absolutely no sign of mousse in his hair nor had he stunk to high heaven of any kind of men's cologne. No, Luke just naturally exuded everything that was masculine.

And all that was feminine in her cried out in response, which was really stupid. Did she have no self-protective instincts at all? Had she learned nothing from her marriage?

While she waited she thought about Carolyn. As far as she knew, Luke was a bachelor. Wade had never spoken about his brother having been married or having any kind of previous entanglement of the female kind—which Luke obviously had had since Carolyn existed—but then again, Wade hadn't been one to speak much. Flex his biceps, yes. Talk, no. There'd been a time in her life when a guy's pecs were recommendation enough to pursue a relationship. She'd naively assumed a well-built body wouldn't embarrass itself by anything less than a sterling interior. Thank God she'd grown past all that.

Luke opened the door just as Marie was beginning to wonder if he'd remembered their appointment.

"Hi," he said.

"Hi," Marie responded as she studied him curiously. He'd been impeccably dressed yesterday when Jason had whacked him. Now here it was, Sunday, almost noon and the man looked, well, disheveled, to be kind.

It was annoying that her heart rhythm picked up anyway. For the life of her, she couldn't come up with an adequate reason why. His jeans were old, frayed, with his knees showing through the few remaining horizontal threads still there. He wore a collared white broadcloth shirt, but it was unbuttoned, untucked and wrinkled. The shirt was short-sleeved and his arms emerged from them thick, heavily muscled and furred. Dark hair curled out from the top of his undershirt, letting Marie know his chest was also furred. If she hadn't seen his hair yesterday, she'd think he hadn't combed it in a month of Sundays, so unkempt did it appear now. And Luke's feet were bare. Bare. Marie shook her head. It was discouraging and ridiculous in equal parts that her heart still lurched at the sight of him. The vision of him now just didn't fit with yesterday's image. Nothing about him did.

Would the real Luke Deforest please stand up?

"Come in," he invited, rather formally Marie thought, considering his attire.

Today's Luke Deforest was living proof of the old adage that clothes did not make the man. Messed and mussed, this was still one fine-looking specimen of the male variety.

Marie became determined not to show any signs of her discomfiture. "Thank you," she replied, nodding acceptance of his invitation and stepping regally, she hoped, into Luke's foyer. She had to thread her way around several shopping bags from stores whose names were familiar to her from her own trips to the mall. She recognized some of the bags from yesterday.

Calypso music drifted in from the back of the house.

Her eyes adjusted to the dimmer interior lighting.

The exterior of the house had been impressive. A warm-colored brick, the large two-story house sat on a wide, deep lot. The landscaping was minimal, a sign of both the newness of the home and its current owner's disinterest in gardening, Marie suspected.

The inside appeared spacious and expensively if unimaginatively finished, with lots of moldings and wide, thick, intricate woodwork throughout. From what Marie could see, all of it seemed to be painted a basic, unimaginative white.

Luke led her through a very masculine-looking living room with white walls and tan carpeting accented by a supple black leather L-shaped sectional. The pink satin-bound blanket from yesterday and a stuffed green bunny about a foot and a half tall lay obtrusively on the couch and Dr. Seuss books lay on the brass-and-glass coffee table before it. Matching brass-and-glass end tables supported black lamps with black shades. They passed through the room, which had little by way of actual decoration, into—she wouldn't have thought it was possible—an even more masculine study.

"Hang on a second," Luke muttered and Marie stood, waiting until he came back with a kitchen chair for her to sit on. He placed the chair behind the massive glass-topped black desk, next to his brass-nail-studded black leather and far more professional chair.

He sank, rather gratefully Marie thought, into his chair

and waved her into the other. "Sit," he said and ran a hand through his hair, making it stand up all the more. "If I remember right from last night, we've got maybe ten or fifteen minutes before the movie ends. When I went to get your chair Ariel had already given up her voice to become human and the king of the mer-people was being turned into a newt or something equally repulsive by this evil overweight octopus. I've got to admit the octopus is pretty awesome, but I'm telling you, it's wearing thin. The whole thing is wearing very thin. Hell, I've had the kid for less than twenty-four hours and I've already got the damn movie practically memorized."

Marie was confused. Why was he so unfamiliar with his daughter and how come she'd never heard about Carolyn before? A long-ago divorce? How long ago could it have been with Carolyn being so young? How often did Luke get to see her? There had to be a mom somewhere, but where and how did she fit into the picture? After all, it took two to tango and Carolyn was living proof Luke knew how to dance.

"Are you divorced?" she asked. "Do you just get Carolyn certain weekends a month or something like that?"

Luke scrubbed his face with his hands. "I wish. No, it's nothing easy like that. Carolyn's mother died a little while ago. It'd been a while since I'd last seen her. Took them a while to track me down, I guess. Carolyn's here to stay and neither one of us is at all sure how we feel about that."

See? She was right. Men were jerks. Except for her grandfather who'd always been there for her, but he was a lot older. Maybe they improved with age. Sort of like cheese. Then again, didn't some varieties just get stinkier the older they got?

"You're the child's father and you haven't bothered to have any contact with her before now?" she questioned incredulously, forgetting in her ire how very large he was.

"They had to track you down to inform you of her mother's death? What kind of a man are you?"

"A tired one," Luke informed her grimly. "A very tired one. Carolyn refused to stay in her own bed last night. She kept climbing in with me. And let me tell you, that child has the boniest elbows and knees you'll ever run into. I know. I ran into them consistently and constantly all night long. Most restless sleeper in town, no, on the continent. No joke. She got me once in the throat. I couldn't breathe. Thought I was going to die."

"You evidently survived the ordeal," Marie said without a great deal of sympathy. She was amazed by the man's total lack of sensitivity. "I'm sure she's just feeling insecure. For heaven's sake, Luke, her mother just died and she's been shuffled off to a father she doesn't even know."

Luke half rose out of his chair and pointed his finger at her. "Listen, lady, you don't know what—" He stopped in midsentence, paused, shook his head, then sat back down. "No, never mind. It's nobody's business but Carolyn's and mine. Just trust me on this. There are things I'm not free to discuss here. They're between Carolyn and me and we're the ones who'll work them out. I hope." He'd muttered that last and Marie barely caught it.

Puzzled, she stared at him. Luke Deforest, the man who only yesterday looked like he could take on the world and win suddenly looked like he'd gone a couple of rounds more than he should have. The man looked defeated. Marie felt the tug on her heartstrings and was confused and angered. He pulled on her in so many different ways how was she supposed to stay uninvolved here? Well, she'd done her share of mothering for this month. Maternal instincts, sexual instincts and any other kind of instincts that had her thinking about jumping on the bandwagon here were just going to have to forget it. Marie was currently unavailable. Jason was enough to deal with. She wasn't going to take on Luke and his defenseless little daughter.

She was getting going while the going was good.

Once again Marie tried to rise. "It certainly sounds like you've got your hands full so I'll just get out of your way. You're not ready to leave and I'm sure the insurance company can deliver the loaner car to you if you ask. Here, I stopped and picked this up on the way over." She tried to hand him a copy of the police report she'd filed. "I'll leave this here for you to look over and I wrote down my phone number and insurance information so you can—"

"Daddy?"

If Marie hadn't been looking right at him, she wouldn't have noticed the slight recoil.

"Yes, Carolyn?"

"All done."

"The movie's over already?"

In other circumstances, Marie would have laughed at the look of sheer panic Luke wore. She was sure he'd never admit it, but he was so obviously clueless as far as how to entertain the child that it was almost funny. Funny in the abstract, that was. Funny only until you took a good look at the little girl. Yesterday Carolyn's face had been buried in Marie's chest. When the child had finally fallen asleep in her car seat, her features had been red, swollen and splotchy from crying.

Today, well my goodness, today Carolyn was a beautiful child not yet a yard tall with crooked wheat-colored pigtails cascading in curls to her shoulders and soft brown eyes framed with embarrassingly long lashes. There was a spattering of freckles running over her cheeks and bridging her nose. As Carolyn's top teeth bit into her quivering yet pink perfect lower lip, Marie noted those teeth were small, white and charmingly askew. Luke would drop a quick five grand straightening those in a few years, Marie decided.

Oh, God, Carolyn was still virtually a baby and she was so forlorn and lonely-looking as she stood there uncertainly in the doorway. So lost and vulnerable appearing as she looked to Luke for guidance as to what to do next in this foreign house with this foreign dad in this foreign town.

Marie's heart went out to the little waif. Marie was a goner.

Not liking this situation didn't change it.

"It's almost lunchtime," Luke finally suggested hopefully after staring nonplussed for several seconds. "How about if I open a can of tuna fish and put it on whole wheat bread? Doesn't that sound good?"

Marie did a double take and stared at him. He was kidding, right?

"Do we got any hot dogs? I like hot dogs," the child offered hopefully.

"A hot dog." Luke raked a hand through his hair. He'd never get it to lie flat again, Marie suspected. "Let me look. Maybe there's a package in the freezer. A hot dog's protein. Sort of," he mumbled to himself. "But there ought to be vegetables. Kids need vegetables to grow right." He snapped his fingers. "A salad. We could have salad."

Marie shook her head. Luke was lost, no doubt about it. No two-year-old worthy of the name would willingly eat salad. The man was definitely out of his milieu. Of course it would be a month or two before he'd admit it.

"Uh, Luke?"

"Yeah, what?"

"What about grapes or a banana? Don't you have some fruit you could cut up for Carolyn?"

"Yeah, I suppose." He frowned as he mentally reviewed his grocery supplies. "Maybe."

Tactfully Marie suggested, "That might be a better choice than salad. Maybe you could convince her to try a little bit of carrot if you cut it up into matchstick size, but you might want to hold off on the salad for a little while." Like twenty years.

Luke frowned and studied the tot. "I don't want her to develop bad eating habits."

"No, no, of course not," Marie quickly assured. "But it would be all right to work up to salad, wouldn't it? I mean, you could start with cooked carrots with a little brown sugar on them and go from there, couldn't you?"

Luke picked up the paper clips from the holder on his desktop and began pouring the clips from hand to hand and back. "I don't know. I'm still not sure about this hot dog thing, either."

"It might be easier. Just for today, you know. Until Carolyn's a little more at home, that is." Marie gave the guy a month, two tops. She, too, had prepared only nutritious balanced meals and snacks when she'd first taken over responsibility for Jason. There'd been a lot of tension, unhappiness, and sneaking out to the local fast-food burger place with friends until Marie had finally caved. She'd never regretted sinking to PB and J and pizza. The peace alone was worth it. Now she slipped him his grains and oatmeal in cookie format, his milk and calcium in pudding or tapioca. Veggies were still a sore point, but life, if not perfect, had at least been salvaged from the proverbial toilet, which was about all you could hope for with an adolescent on the premises, Marie had decided.

At the time, Marie had had her epiphany. She'd discovered that all of life was a balancing act, a compromise if you will. Luke would eventually discover the same truth, but it needn't be quite the same rough journey she'd made.

"Then maybe, after lunch, if she doesn't need to nap, you could take her to a park. There must be one around here somewhere."

"Kiddie Kingdom's not too far," Luke said, thinking out loud. "That's not a bad idea. Then maybe she could watch another movie while I got some work done. I've still got to unpack those few boxes they sent along with her and I bought her some stuff for her room, sheets and things that match, more for a little girl, you know? Barbie. My sisters used to play with her and what's his name—Kevin, Kent, whatever. Amazing, but she's still around. It's all still in bags in the front hall.''

She'd noticed the bags. The front hall was probably right where Jason had dropped them. They'd made no progress since then. Marie rubbed her nose and considered the possibility that the bags' lack of progress might be partially her fault. If Luke was frazzled, their accidental meeting yesterday might have something—not a lot—but something to do with it. She guessed it wouldn't kill her to at least come up with a plan of action before she left.

"That's a good plan," Marie agreed tactfully. "But instead of another movie, after they deliver your car why don't you stop at a home improvement place—you know, one of those glorified hardware stores—on the way home from the park and get a sandbox, a slew of sand, a bucket and a shovel? Then she could be playing actively instead of sitting passively while you work."

Luke's posture visibly straightened. He was definitely perking up. "That's another decent idea, Marie. Thank you. I'd have eventually thought of it myself, of course, but this is good. Maybe a swing set, too. Kids like those, don't they? Maybe I'll get one of those fancy ones with a fort on one end and the sandbox underneath. There's a house down at the end of the block with one like that."

"They take time to assemble," Marie warned. "It certainly won't be done any time today. But I bet Carolyn would enjoy helping you open the packages you've got in the front hall and arranging her room with you."

Luke was in a fever. Marie expected him to start taking notes any minute, although he kept his tone cool. "That's good, Marie, that's really good. I appreciate your input. Now, what do we do after that?"

What, he expected a minute-by-minute itinerary for the next fifteen years or so until Carolyn went away to college? Good grief. She thought fast. "Well, uh, walk up to the grocery store and get whatever you need for dinner. Walk-

ing will eat up some time and it's good exercise for her.
Help wear her out a bit for tonight, you know.'' That should
make it more appealing to him. ''Stop in the school supply
aisle and get her some construction paper, um, crayons—''
Marie waved her hand expressively ''—whatever else you
see that looks interesting. She can color or mush that kiddie
dough stuff while you get dinner ready. Hands-on experiences are very important for her age,'' Marie concluded,
hoping she sounded like she knew what she was talking
about.

Luke was all admiration. ''That is brilliant, absolutely
brilliant.'' He gave Marie a calculating look. ''I don't suppose you'd be willing to—''

Marie concentrated on looking regretful. ''Gee, I wish I
could stay and help, Luke, but I've got to get back. Can't
leave an adolescent on his own too long. You never know
what he'll get up to. Why, right this minute he's—'' Marie
swallowed her words as she thought. She wasn't about to
admit Jason wasn't even home just then. ''That is to
say—''

But Luke wasn't leapfrogging his way up the corporate
ladder for nothing. He'd caught her slight hesitation, understood its meaning and pounced. ''He's what?''

''He's at an audio equipment store with a friend who's
already got his license drooling over this outrageously expensive surround sound system he's pressuring me to buy,''
Marie admitted glumly. She'd checked out how long his
friend had had his license and made sure Jason was the
only other kid going to be in the car but still, she'd known
letting Jason go out was a bad idea and here was the proof.
She had no excuse now not to stick around and help Luke
out.

Not only did she doubt it would be properly appreciated,
she also had the issue of her own self-survival to consider.

Plain and simple, she didn't want to be around Luke
Deforest. He was too darn virile. Too appealing to that core

of womanly essence deep inside her—the core she'd been sure had died an unnatural death a couple of months back. Marie shook her head in sorrow over her pitiful state. Basically, Luke made her ache. He made her yearn for things. Impossible things she'd long given up on having.

Luke was speaking. Marie shook her head to clear it and tried to catch up.

"—top of the line. We'll have to get him over here and let him watch a movie or something—"

"You have surround sound?"

Luke gave her a puzzled look. "Isn't that what I was just saying?"

"Do you have one of those subwoofer things?" Marie asked suspiciously.

"Yeah, sure. Of course."

Marie slapped her thigh with her hand. She knew it. She just knew it. It was obviously a male thing. Some defect in the Y chromosome. She'd been right all along in her decision to have nothing further to do with the male half of the human race, relatives unfortunately excluded.

"You pwitty."

Marie's internal diatribe disturbed, she looked down. Little Carolyn had edged her way over and now stood right in front of her. Marie smiled. "Not half as pretty as you, sweetie."

Carolyn turned to Luke for confirmation. "Her pwitty."

Luke studied Marie for a disconcertingly long time before responding. "Yes, honey, she is. Very pretty."

Marie couldn't control her blush.

Carolyn caught Marie by the pant leg and didn't appear inclined to let go. "Her have a hot dog too, Daddy?"

Luke smiled, a bit evilly in Marie's opinion. "Absolutely. All we have to do is convince her to stay. Why don't you ask her? I bet Auntie Marie couldn't turn down a sugarplum like you."

"Oh, all right," Marie said, giving in. "I'll stay. Just for a while. But I want the tuna fish on whole wheat." And her capitulation had absolutely nothing to do with wanting to spend more time with Luke. Absolutely nothing.

Chapter Three

For a large man, Luke could move. He jumped from his chair, startling Marie. It was almost as though he didn't want to give her time to change her mind. But that made no sense. He'd never made any pretense of liking her.

Then he said, "Tuna on wheat. Got it. Everybody out to the kitchen. Hup, two, three, four."

Carolyn reached up and took Marie's hand as they dutifully followed the leader. "Now," Luke inquired scant minutes later as he waved the tin of fish in the air. "What do you want in the tuna? Pickle relish? Onions? Celery seed?" He'd found the appropriate can in the cabinet, the electric opener was at hand and raring to go. He even attempted a smile and Marie found those particular muscles hadn't totally atrophied since yesterday afternoon after all. They still worked.

"Celery, the real kind not just its seeds, a *small* amount of onion—" not that she was going to be kissing anybody except maybe Carolyn "—and mayo, thank you," Marie replied primly. Celery seed? Yuck. "And I want my bread toasted, please."

Luke waved two slices of whole wheat across the room in the general direction of the counter with the toaster before handing the bread to her. "There you go."

"Thanks," she muttered dryly and wondered why Mr. Gracious had bothered to invite her at all. He never had been Mr. Hospitality. Ah, well, she was used to taking care of herself—and anybody else who came along. She could handle it.

Luke had heard the unspoken criticism in her tone but he didn't bother to acknowledge it. None of his present circumstances were any of his doing. None. And he was not feeling the least bit gracious. "Milk, pop, juice in the fridge. The cups are in the cabinet over the dishwasher."

Marie sighed as she dropped the bread into the toaster slots and pushed the lever down before going in search of the glasses. "Don't have many guests, eh, Mr. Deforest? Your manners appear to be a tad rusty."

"Ms. Ferguson, you did not pick a happy time to have your uncle ram my car. I'm feeling just a little bit persecuted myself right now and quite frankly, am not up to doing the congenial host bit. Now, Carolyn appears to have taken a shine to you and it would be a whole lot easier on me if she was happy sooner rather than later. The way I see it, you owe me. I didn't break your uncle's neck the way I wanted to, after all. And the payback I'd like most of all would be for you to get us on the road to happy familyhood around here. Do that and I will personally buy you the most expensive dinner at the swankiest place in town."

Marie all but snorted. The accident had not been her fault, either. Let Jason teach Luke about the joys of family life. She herself knew only what she'd read about conventional happy families. Marie hadn't seen her father since she was five when he'd had a doozy of a midlife crisis and taken off to "find himself." As far as Marie knew, her father was still someplace out there hot on his own trail.

Her mom had taken to drinking to fill the void. She'd ended up pickling her own internal organs and had died of cirrhosis of the liver.

Marie had been raised by her grandfather and stepgrandmother Pearl from the time she'd been eight. Jason had come along a year later. Pearl was much younger than her grandfather but still old for a first-time mother. She'd concentrated so hard on acquiring newborn parenting skills that she'd given Marie enough room to run a bit wild. Still, Marie gave Pearl credit. She hadn't treated Marie like Cinderella. Not at all. In fact, Pearl had been a sweetheart who'd tried hard to never take undue advantage of her nontraditionally structured family's built in baby-sitter. Then, two years ago, Pearl had died. Breast cancer hadn't been detected until it was too late. Sometimes it seemed to Marie that she'd spent her entire life dealing with desertion and or death.

Her grandfather had always been there for her, bless his cantankerous, irreverent heart. He was a rock, but even rocks eventually wore down. Grandpa still struggled to do his best, but he was seventy-five now and no longer spry. It was taking his bones forever to knit themselves back together after this last fall. Marie would cut out her tongue before admitting it to anyone, but sometimes she was so scared. What if her grandfather never got his strength back? Who would she have then to help her deal with Jason? No one. It was a scary thought.

Marie refused to allow herself to dwell on the possibility. She'd made a conscientious decision to simply take each day as it came. The tables were now turned. It was payback time. Grandpa needed her care and her help raising his son. Marie wasn't like her mother or father. Admittedly there had been a few years when Marie had been momentarily, uh, dazzled by life on the edge, but basically she believed in responsibility. She could delay finding herself for a few more years. Provided she lived through this current period with her mental faculties still intact.

Marie's expression softened as she watched Carolyn carefully dunk diced hot dog chunks into the blob of ketchup Luke had dabbed onto her plate. Now this little sweetie was a piece of cake compared to Jason. The adolescent mind was a foreign land with few landmarks recognizable to anyone outside of the ages fourteen through about twenty. You did what you could to get them through this period alive. Psychological damage didn't matter. So long as they were still breathing by the time they hit twenty or so, which was a definite challenge in and of itself, they could go see a shrink to undo any emotional damage you'd done in an effort to ensure mere physical survival of the species.

Of course by then, you were in major need of a shrink yourself.

Marie smiled fondly down. Yes indeed, this little munchkin would be easy. All she really needed to flourish for the next ten or twelve years until she hit the dreaded fourteen was lots of hugs and kisses, large and small muscle activities, and plenty of sleep and food. Marie had no doubt that with that combination little Carolyn would grow and flourish just like a weed.

Luke became almost affable during lunch and to Marie's surprise, he had some decent knock-knock jokes he shared with Carolyn, who didn't get them at all. Marie, however, found herself chuckling a time or two. It was interesting to watch the tension leak out of him as the meal progressed. What did he have to be so stressed about? And why did he keep looking at Marie with those narrowed, considering eyes?

Carolyn munched contentedly on her hot dog pieces, banana chunks, and the scant handful of pretzels her miserly father had provided. She was tucked into a spot between

the two adults and continually glanced from one to the
other as if in need of reassurance that they were still there.

"More pwetzels? Pweez, Daddy?"

Marie watched in amusement as Luke nudged a small
pile of matchstick carrots closer. "First finish your milk
and eat some of these yummy carrots. Then we'll see."

Marie narrowed her eyes as the ploy worked. Maybe if
you got them young enough...hmm. Of course, she'd eat
anything Luke prepared for her, too. Even if he just got it
out of the bag for you, there was something about Luke
that made you want to cooperate. Heck, the average female
would be so mesmerized by Luke himself, she probably
wouldn't even realize what she were doing until the deed
was done. What a sad, sad commentary on the female of
the species—to be so easily duped.

Carolyn seemed happy with the graham cracker she got
for dessert—the young were so refreshingly naive and innocent, weren't they? After cleaning up, they piled into
Marie's car and headed for Kiddie Kingdom. Kiddie Kingdom just happened to be right across the street from Po-
tawatami Zoo, an act of serendipity if ever there was one.

Carolyn chattered the whole way home. "She's worn me
out," Luke admitted with a groan after releasing Carolyn's
restraints and lifting the child out.

"Me, too," Marie agreed and laughed when she couldn't
restrain a yawn. "I really have to go now," she added.
"My grandfather's grass needs cutting. Jason was supposed
to do it when he got back from ogling the displays at Media
Central. I don't understand this subwoofer fixation of his,
but I suppose it's better than finding girlie magazines hidden around the house."

"As far as Jason's concerned, it's probably a toss-up
between the lingerie catalog, the car magazines and the
electronic supply warehouse," Luke decided after briefly
considering the age of the subject involved.

Marie made a mental note to go through the catalogs

stacked on the sofa table in their small family room and pull anything involving underwear or lingerie. "You're probably right. At any rate, I told him I was only going to ask once because I was tired of arguing every time I ask him to do something. If it didn't get done, I said I'd do it myself but then I wouldn't take him driving again for at least a week."

Luke's eyes widened. "Whoa, we're talking hardball here."

Marie was immediately defensive. "Well, I am tired of arguing."

Luke held up his hands, palms out. "I'm not disagreeing."

"The thing is, I know he'll sulk for a while before he caves. At least until after the sun goes down so the neighbors will think I'm mean and evil for making him do it in the dark. I want to get home and cut it first so I have the next week free of experiences similar to the one I shared with you yesterday. My nerves can't handle a whole lot more. I'm about to lose it, no joke. I need the week off. At the rate things are going, I'll be twenty-five and look fifty— provided I live to see my next birthday at all."

Luke stuck his hands in his pants pocket and jiggled his change while he studied her. He had stumbled onto a good thing here. He'd dreaded this afternoon, his first alone with Carolyn. In fact, the anticipation of it had caused him to wake up in a cold sweat around two in the morning. What did he know about entertaining a two-year-old—for the rest of her life? But instead of a nightmare, it had been a dream and—he'd never admit it out loud—mostly due to Marie.

Marie had converted his darkest fears into, well, maybe not a fantasy, but at least a story with the possibility of a happy ending. The only fly in the ointment he could see was, well, his unrelenting attraction for Marie. It was a problem he'd always had around her but she'd been married to his brother and totally off-limits. He'd resented the effect

she had on him back then and he resented it now. And
Marie had problems. He'd only suspected as much when
he'd first met her. His analysis had been based solely on
the fact she was married to his brother and surely only an
idiot would marry another idiot. If it wasn't for Carolyn,
he'd continue to steer a course well clear of Marie.

But there was Carolyn. His attraction to Marie was certainly an inconvenience, one he'd have to keep hidden as
he did not want Marie aware of the effect she had on him.
But he'd be willing to put up with any amount of physical
discomfort and consider it a fair exchange for a little guidance with Carolyn.

And Marie was turning out to be somewhat of a surprise.
He'd enjoyed their time together this afternoon. It was beginning to look like Marie had depths beneath that souped-
up exterior Luke hadn't suspected. Wade had probably died
ignorant of them. Luke didn't really understand it, but before Marie had arrived, if that mermaid had broken into
song one more time, he swore to heaven and all its saints
that he'd have had to kill himself. Once Marie had been on
the scene he'd actually felt himself softening toward both
calypso and the little sap's plight.

And Luke Deforest wasn't stupid. No sir. He knew how
to cut a deal.

"Tell you what," he said consideringly. "You help me
help Carolyn get her room in order and I'll go back to your
place with you. I'll cut the grass and pay for the dinner-
making supplies. All you have to do is suffer our company
a little bit longer." No way would he admit it out loud, but
Luke was not ready to be left on his own just yet. He'd cut
Marie's lawn plus ten of her closest neighbors' to avoid it.
What was another few hours of dealing with the nagging
discomfort of his arousal compared to the difficulty of
keeping Carolyn happy on his own?

While Marie had opened his eyes to the possibility he
might actually survive his fatherhood experience, he was

yet to be totally convinced. The whole thing really was completely unfair. And there was something about Marie that plainly and simply made him feel more alive. It might make him mad to lose his much vaunted control but there was no denying that there were certain parts of his body that were showing more vigor for a longer, extended period of time than he'd had to deal with since he was sixteen and had himself kept old lingerie catalogs secreted between the box spring and mattress for reference.

Coming at a time when Luke had been convinced life as he knew it was over, he was reluctant to let go of that renewed feeling of vigor. "So, what do you think?"

Marie considered the proposition from all angles. She *really* hated cutting the grass. With a passion she hated it. Changing the sheets up in Carolyn's room to a more juvenile set was no big deal, far preferable to dealing with lawn clippings. Besides, she'd get to admire Luke's superb physique a little bit longer. The self-propel on Grandpa's mower didn't always work. Luke might get all hot and sweaty. He might even take off his shirt. And there was no harm in looking, was there? It seemed like a win-win deal to her. Marie hadn't gotten much of a toehold in the working world before she'd come running back home and then taken over Jason's care but she'd learned enough to know she ought to at least appear to be reluctant.

"I had intended to make some oatmeal cookies later on or maybe peanut butter. I hadn't quite decided yet. I suppose Carolyn might enjoy helping stir the batter."

Luke felt relief sweep through him. The woman was a gold mine of ideas. A virtual gold mine. He barely managed to refrain from slapping his thigh in glee. "Maybe" was all he was willing to commit to out loud while he made a mental note to watch Carolyn's intake of the finished product. Then he posted another mental note to find a book somewhere on the nutritional needs of children. The library might have something. He'd try there first. Luke could virtually feel hives threatening to erupt at the mere thought of facing the bookstore at the mall again so soon after his last sojourn there.

It took a little over three hours to whip the new bedroom into shape, mostly because they were working around Carolyn. The time would have been halved if they'd put the tot in front of the television and gone at it without her, quartered if Marie had tackled it on her own. It wasn't that Marie had to redo anything Luke had accomplished with regard to Carolyn's room. No, the problem was far more embarrassing. She kept finding herself staring at him, then realizing that she'd been staring and praying that Luke hadn't noticed. The man needed a personality transplant after all, and it was a disconcerting failure on her part, to say the least, that she found herself so attracted.

Finally Marie was able to concentrate long enough to make a list of things Luke might want to buy to complete the room's transition. A bookcase for Carolyn's Dr. Seuss library and shelves for the stuffed animals. Some kind of closet organizer. Those kinds of things.

By the time they left Luke's residence, Carolyn was holding her hand and chattering like a magpie. Half of it Marie understood, the rest was a little too convoluted to decipher. It didn't bother Carolyn. The child jabbered contentedly away and didn't balk until she saw Marie heading to a different auto than she and Luke. Luke's rental had been delivered while they'd labored. Carolyn set up a fuss and let go of her hand only long enough to attach herself to Marie's leg where she hung like a limpet.

"She wants to ride with you," Luke informed her, stating the obvious.

Marie knelt down. "Sweetie, you have to ride with Daddy. You have to be in your car seat so you'll be safe."

Luke considered his options. As he saw it, he could go for peace and quiet and play the odds Marie wouldn't have an accident. Chances were good nothing would happen, after all. His parents had never buckled him in as a child. Seat belts had been a novelty back then and he was still around. A lot of people his age and older were still around. Or, he could play it safe, strap Carolyn in properly and deal with her carrying on the whole way over.

No contest.

"Sorry, pumpkin, but you need to climb into your chair and let Daddy buckle you in. We'll be there before you know it and then Auntie Marie's going to bake cookies with you. Won't that be fun?" Luke fast-talked his daughter right into the car and into her seat. He quickly slid behind the steering wheel before Carolyn even realized she'd been finessed.

Carolyn bounced in her chair and chanted, "Cookie, cookie, cookie!"

"That's right, a cookie for my little cupcake," Luke agreed, and grimaced. He sounded like a moron. He shook his head in disparagement at how low his life had sunk and started the engine of his rental car. "I'll follow you," he said out his window and Marie nodded in agreement.

She was pleased with the way Luke had handled Carolyn's budding temper. The child's safety had come first. With a little guidance Luke and his daughter just might make it, after all.

Her good mood deteriorated as soon as her grandfather's house came into view. Jason, the creep, was out cutting the grass! He had to pick today of all times to be agreeable? Now she was going to have to take him out driving again. It would be a major miracle if she didn't develop a nervous twitch and ulcers before her next birthday, Marie decided.

She parked out on the street and glowered at the scene through her windshield. If that wasn't just like a teenager. They'd do anything to make you crazy—including cooperate when you least expected it.

Luke set Carolyn on the sidewalk, then walked across the parkway to open Marie's door. "Looks like he took your threat seriously,'' he commented through her open window.

"No kidding," Marie said with a scowl. "Humph." She folded her arms across her chest. "Look at that. Probably blowing his eardrums out with whatever he's got blasting on those headphones, mowing away as though he didn't have a care in the world. Darn his hide, he's even doing a decent job just to spite me."

Luke had to hide a grin at that. "Yeah, it looks like he's determined not to leave you any outs."

"Like I couldn't see right through his scheme," she mumbled as she climbed irritably out of the car. "Like this isn't the first time in recorded history he's done it willingly and right."

Luke turned his head and managed to stifle a laugh. "I'll make a deal with you. You make dinner for Carolyn and me the way we originally planned and *I'll* take Jason out driving some time this week." Unfortunately, his gaze fell to her mouth while he made his offer. God, he really hated this. He really was going to have to kiss the woman and in all likelihood it would have to be some time soon.

Caught up in wondering how those pouting lips of hers might taste, Luke didn't notice that Marie had stopped in her tracks and was staring at him, stunned.

"You'd do that?"

He decided to make her nervous and pretended to reconsider. "Well, I don't know. How good of a cook are you?"

"I can beat a hot dog."

Luke nodded. "Then I'd do that."

Marie stood right on her grandfather's parkway in full view of any neighbors who might have been looking, as well as an impressionable uncle and a toddler, and kissed her personality-challenged former brother-in-law. Then she found herself thinking seriously about giving him a second kiss. Luke might not be real personable, but the man had lips. Then she glanced at little Carolyn, who had come over and begun yanking on Luke's pant leg.

"Daddy?"

"Yes, Carolyn?"

While Luke tried to translate what turned out to be a request to go see the doggie next door Marie reluctantly gave up the idea of an instant repeat of their kiss and stepped back.

The surprise of Marie's kiss had fogged Luke's brain. It took longer than it should have to translate Carolyn's gibberish and deny the request to pat a strange animal.

Then he put in some time dissecting what had just happened. He'd just kissed Wade's widow, for heaven's sake. As he thought about his brother now, he realized it wouldn't be kind to say Wade had been reckless as a youth, but it would be the truth. Wade had stayed that way through adolescence, as well. Luke had spent a lot of time saving his little brother from situations of his own making. His parents had washed their hands of Wade by the time he'd been sixteen. Luke had had hopes Wade would eventually mature but when Wade had gotten married at age twenty, Luke had made the decision to back off. If Wade was old enough to get married, he was old enough to live by his choices. Why a reasonably sane woman like Marie had made the choice to marry Wade, was another question entirely.

Unfortunately for Luke, his new and unexpected role as pappa had him just about desperate for somebody who knew anything about young children; young girl children to be specific. From what he'd seen so far, Marie fit the bill. Serendipity had brought them together and Luke was determined it would take them a whole heck of a lot further. He was going to pick her brain until he knew everything she knew about kids and give her a few tips on the inner workings of the male adolescent in exchange. Then he'd walk away. Luke was absolutely not going to allow himself to move in on his brother's ex-wife. He was tired of saving people, tired of nurturing. Anybody could see Marie had a lot of needs. Getting involved with someone like her would just be complicated. And here stood a man whose life needed no further complications.

Decision made, Luke decided he was not above using a child to help him keep sight of his goals. Luke picked up Carolyn and held her in his arms to keep himself from grabbing Marie and repeating the kiss. Not that there would have been any serious danger in a second taste. It would have been just a test, you know? All in the name of science. It was possible Marie had been scuffling her feet and the zap he'd felt had been simply the result of static electricity or something. August was a little early in the year for the air to be that dry, but you never knew. What he did know was that Marie's brief peck hadn't cured his lower body ache. As a matter of fact, if he wasn't real careful here, he could end up walking doubled over by the end of the evening. Luke took a deep breath and blew it out to a measured count of ten.

"Thank you, thank you, thank you," Marie gushed while Luke juggled Carolyn and made a conscious attempt to straighten back up.

Luke nodded recognition of her gratitude. Yes, he'd chosen the right card to play. Jason was her weak spot. She was as lost in dealing with him as he was with Carolyn. Hell, he should have made the offer as soon as Jason hit him yesterday, saved himself a sleepless night. Truth be told, this almost made the dent in his candy-apple-red pride and joy less psychologically hurtful to him.

Marie felt her tingling lips with a fingertip and studied Luke's mouth. She threw caution to the winds. To heck with setting a good example. Arching her body so as not to smush Carolyn, she reached up, pulled Luke's head down and gave him another smacker.

Luke wondered if all driver's ed instructors got this kind of reaction?

If so, it was possible he'd made the wrong career choice.

Then again they said you were never too old for a career move.

Next Luke wondered what Marie would do if he offered to take over the task entirely. Throw her entire body at him? It might be worth the trouble for a serious taste of her. But no, Luke was a careful man by nature. He'd have to experience both the driving and a whole lot more of the kissing before he made a decision like that.

Mostly for something to do other than stare at Marie's mouth, Luke said, "Let's get her in the house. That dog next door is too great a temptation for a two-year-old to pass up. You think he'd bite?"

Marie let herself be steered up the front walk. His hand in the center of her back felt too good to fight. "It seems friendly enough," she said consideringly. "But I'm certainly not going to trust Carolyn's safety to my initial impression of an animal that big with that number of sharp teeth."

"Me, either," Luke muttered in agreement.

While Marie fumbled with her keys she wondered if she shouldn't be listening to her own advice. Luke was very large and had a full set of beautiful pearly white choppers. She sure hoped she wasn't about to become his dinner.

Marie pushed the door open and closed her eyes at the first rush of cooler, air-conditioned air. The familiar lemon smell and the sight of the hall stand overflowing with mail relaxed her. This was her home. The place she'd grown up. The rooms in the older home were relatively small and there was a lot of woodwork, all of it stained dark. Some psychologist would probably have a field day analyzing the sense of security she felt here and comparing her return to her grandparents' house to a subconscious return to the womb. Whatever. It worked for her.

"Come on in," Marie invited. "The kitchen's back this way. We might as well get started on supper. I know Jason. He'll be starving when he comes back inside. I've got the makings for sloppy joes."

Ten minutes later she was browning ground beef with Luke hanging over her shoulder and Carolyn's head swiveling to track her every step. Marie felt decidedly claustrophobic.

Luke watched intently. He'd lived on his own a long time now. He could scramble an egg, take a preformed burger out of the freezer and fry it up, but basically, that was about it. Most recipes ended up serving four to six. He'd noticed that early on. It had never seemed worthwhile to cook for himself. Not when he'd have to eat the same thing every night for almost a week to get rid of it. When he wanted something fancier than a sandwich or burger, he got carryout.

But he couldn't do that with a child in the house. They needed regular, cooked-at-home food. And not just macaroni and cheese. Luke wondered if Marie knew how to make meat loaf or maybe even pot roast? He kept careful track of the types of pots Marie was using. He was going to have to go out and buy some and needed to know what shapes and sizes were appropriate. The skillet she was using appeared to be about three inches deep, maybe ten across. And the pot happily spitting steam on the back burner was maybe six inches deep, eight across. Marie lowered the flame under the skillet, turned the handle in so that no little hands could grab it and pull it down on themselves, then went into the pantry.

Luke followed, hot on her heels.

"Now what are you doing?"

Marie was seriously thinking about hyperventilating. It seemed the only logical response to being trapped in a closet with Luke Deforest. "Getting an onion," she said.

"Oh."

She felt like apologizing for boring her guest but what the heck was he expecting? Marie was a good basic chef. Sloppy joes, pot roast, chicken and dumplings—stuff like that. If Luke had been envisioning exotic spices or ground beef flambé, he was in for a major disappointment. "I'm also getting the barbecue sauce," she offered. Maybe he'd find that more exciting.

But Luke just nodded seriously as if he were keeping a mental inventory of her every ingredient. Was he afraid she didn't know what she was doing and would accidentally add something inappropriate? Maybe he thought she was going to poison him. Well, she might, Marie thought a little huffily, and Jason was certainly a candidate as well, but surely Luke knew he could trust her not to harm little Carolyn.

God, she couldn't breathe. "Listen, Luke," Marie said. "How about if you and Carolyn, uh, set the table?" The table was on the other side of the kitchen. Certainly she'd be able to get her air better with him a room's breadth away.

Luke was disappointed. He could hardly say no, but how was he supposed to learn how to create a dinner for Carolyn from way over there? Besides, Marie was evidently not the type to get real blatant with her perfume and he doubted he'd be able pick up the hint of raspberry she wore from across the room. He shrugged and tried to be philosophical. Well, at least the temptation to stick his nose in her hair and take a good whiff of whatever great smelling shampoo she used would be alleviated. His neck could only stretch so far, after all.

He had to remind himself that keeping a distance would be for the best. "Which drawer's hiding the silverware?" Luke nodded at Marie's gesture. "Come on, Carolyn, push your little stool over here and you can help me count. You know how to count, don't you, sweetie?"

Carolyn nodded vigorously and industriously pushed the

step stool Marie had given her across the floor. She demonstrated her counting while she pushed. "One, two, fwee, five, eight, six—"

"Your education has been sadly neglected, young lady," Luke informed the two-year-old. "We're going to have to see what we can do about that. No more runaway mermaids until you can count properly to ten."

Marie rolled her eyes and went back to dicing onion.

Luke kept his eye on her while he reinforced counting up to four with his daughter. "One, two, three, four. Now you say it while we put the plates on the table."

"One—"

But Luke's attention was fractured. Marie moved so gracefully around the kitchen, he thought. Just look at the way she held the spoon while she sampled her cooking. Nodding to herself, adding another squirt of mustard, a bit more of—what was that? He craned his neck. Oh, brown sugar.

"Two—"

Luke doubted Marie was even aware of how she sashayed from the stove to the pantry and back again.

"Foh—"

Man, with moves like that, she should have been a model. No joke. He could see her now, swaying her way down the runway.

"Fwee. All done, Daddy."

"Hmm? Oh, good job, honey. See? It just takes practice to get it right." Luke patted the top of Carolyn's head while wondering over Marie's muffled chuckle. "Come on, we'll practice some more with the forks and spoons." He'd just have to learn to not notice some things about Marie, Luke decided. Marie was part of the furniture. Part of the furniture. Part of—

Marie couldn't help but wonder what had Luke so distracted that he hadn't noticed his daughter's counting errors. Surely the man knew *fwee* came before *foh* and not after. Marie's humor didn't last long, however. She was really starting to get a little worried. A lot of small things were adding up to the unwanted conclusion that there was something wrong with her. The smell of her bubbling meat mixture was just awful. It was making her ill, yet she knew the meat had been fresh and the ingredients were the same she'd used time and time again. And she was tired all the time. Just look at the way she'd napped most of the way to Kalamazoo yesterday. Heck, she'd be willing to lie down right there and then and take a little snooze.

No, there was something wrong and she was getting a horrible suspicion she knew what that something was.

A few weeks before Wade had died, he'd talked her into attempting a reconciliation. Marie had taken her vows seriously. They'd been young, sophomores in college when they'd married, mostly because they couldn't keep their hands off each other and Marie had been raised as a churchgoer. She'd stayed with Wade quite a while after she suspected the marriage was over trying to make it work. When *he'd* finally left *her* six months ago, she'd come back to the home she'd grown up in. But when he'd called and offered to make a real attempt at working things out, actually see a counselor with her, her grandfather had agreed with her that it would be the right thing to do. Yes, they'd slept together, but she'd made him use protection, not wanting to add a baby to an unstable situation.

"But there was that one time when the condom broke," she muttered to herself as she stood as far away from the stove top as she possibly could while still stirring the sloppy joes. "But it was only the once. Surely—"

But she hadn't had a period since. Initially she'd written it off as stress, but she'd just had her third miss. Then there was the tiredness and the nausea. Brewing coffee that morning had almost killed her until she'd poured it down the drain and opened the windows to air the kitchen out.

And Marie sure didn't want to eat these damn sloppy joes for dinner. She wanted…a good dill pickle.

"You know what else?" Marie asked before hushing herself. *I want Luke.* Yes, indeed. Her entire body was hypersensitive lately. Her breasts were tender and what she really wanted was Luke's hands caressing them.

And she wanted to kiss him.

All over.

Now there was a mental image that had the ache in her breasts picking up tempo.

Good grief, she was losing her mind.

Marie dropped her spoon on the stove top and went to call Jason in. More people in the room, that's what they needed. With a good crowd around her, she'd be just fine. At least that's what she told herself.

Chapter Four

Jason came in reeking of a combination of gasoline, sweat and freshly cut grass. Marie met him with a firm look of implacability that was rapidly becoming second nature to her. "Kick your shoes off. Don't even think about tracking those grass clippings through here."

Jason paused, noted that Luke was watching the byplay and only then stopped to argue rather than ignoring her edict totally. "Just to the sink," he said. "I'm dying of thirst."

Marie held firm. It was a lot easier to do with Luke's hulking presence right behind her. "N-O, no," she said. But she also walked over to the sink herself and filled a tall glass with water. She hand delivered it as Jason was still struggling with the laces on his old sneakers by the time it was full. "Here," she said, offering Jason the cup. "You did a good job out there."

Jason chugged the entire glass down without pausing. He handed it back. "Thanks," he said. His gratitude sounded only slightly begrudging.

Marie took civility any way she could get it from her

uncle. She nodded. "You're welcome. I appreciate that I didn't have to nag." No, she didn't; but it wouldn't do to admit it. She wrinkled her nose. "But you're going to have to wash up before dinner. You smell."

Jason shucked the second shoe and padded across the kitchen floor in socks stained green. "Yeah, yeah, I know. But we're going driving tomorrow, right?"

"Maybe not tomorrow," Marie responded and Jason whirled around ready to jump down her throat. Marie held her hand up in a stopping motion. "But definitely sometime this week. I promise."

"What's wrong with tomorrow?"

"Luke may not have time," Marie said, loving the bomb she was about to drop.

Jason's eyes narrowed as he sensed the trap. He hitched a thumb in Luke's direction. "What's he have to do with our deal?"

"It's turned into a double swap," she informed him with relish. "In return for feeding him and Carolyn tonight, Luke's going to take you driving for me. This will be so much better," Marie assured her uncle with a patently false smile. "You know how you hate driving with me."

"Yeah, sure, you're the pits, but—"

Luke straightened to full height and took a step forward, causing Jason to take a step back.

He also changed his tune. "Yeah, well, fine. Whatever. So long as I get to go, I guess." Then he ignominiously fled the room.

Luke leaned back against the counter and Marie dished up sloppy joes with a smile on her face. She put chips into a second bowl and held a jar of applesauce upside down over a third until the contents had all dumped out. "There," she said, just about satisfied with dinner preparations. She retrieved milk from the refrigerator and set it on the table right in its carton. She'd already dirtied up two extra bowls as it was for the company. Ordinarily she'd have served Jason the applesauce out of the jar and the chips directly out of the bag. She wasn't adding a pitcher to the after-dinner cleanup as well. Not when she knew very well she'd be stuck doing it by herself.

"Dinner is served," Marie announced. She laughed as Luke struggled to seat Carolyn so she wouldn't slide off the phone book he'd appropriated for a booster seat. Marie went to the bottom of the stairs and called up to Jason, letting him know the food was on the table.

"Be right there," he yelled down.

Marie returned to the kitchen. Much to her amazement, Luke seated her. "Thank you," she said and tried to remember the last time she'd been shown even such a small courtesy. Unexpectedly, tears welled and Luke looked at her oddly.

"Something wrong?" he asked, eyes narrowing in suspicion. "Jason say something out of line just now?"

Marie made a helpless little gesture. "No, no, nothing like that. I'm fine. Really, I am." And other than the fact that she was a hairbreadth away from cracking up, she was. It took a few seconds, but Marie managed to get her tear ducts back under control. Relieved, she blinked a few times to clear her eyes. Good grief, she was an emotional wreck. Imagine such a simple courtesy putting her into tears. She was forced to wonder what would happen should Luke hold a door for her or, better yet, bring her flowers. Probably break down and bawl like a baby.

Whoa! Bring her flowers? As if! Where in the wide world had *that* stray thought come from? Some hitherto uncharted area of her brain she'd best get a handle on, Marie decided and sent a mental reminder to all portions of her mind that she'd sworn off men. Any and all synapses whether they handled conscious or unconscious impulses had just better get with the program if they knew what was good for them, too. She was using Luke for her own ends and that was all. Get a few driving lessons, maybe even a

license out of him then drop him, like a hot potato. Period.
Luke was male and she was allergic to the species. Allergic.
She didn't want him holding chairs, doors *or* bringing flowers—not even her favored painted daisies and that was final.

Yes, she did.

Heck.

Marie used half a bun to make a sandwich for Carolyn
and passed it on to Luke for him to portion out the chips
and applesauce as he saw fit. Marie watched out of the
corner of her eye as she fixed two full sandwiches for Luke.
Carolyn got a grand total of three potato chips and a huge
blob of applesauce. She bit her lip to keep from smiling,
then noticed Luke was narrowly eyeing his plate, then the
pot in a calculating manner. Shaking her head, Marie added
a third helping of sloppy joe. Men and their appetites.
Where in the world did they put all those calories? There
was certainly nothing excess hanging around Luke De-
Forest's waist.

"Are you sure there's enough for everyone else?" Luke
asked politely, but the question lacked sincerity, Marie decided as Luke took the plate and began ladling a gallon of
applesauce next to the sloppy joes, making it impossible
for Marie to take one back even if she wanted to.

"No, it's fine," Marie said, shaking her head. "Go right
ahead." She wasn't all that hungry anyway. The smell of
the bubbling meat mixture had made her stomach queasy
and Marie doubted she'd be eating all that much. Maybe
she'd just have the other half of Carolyn's bun.

Jason waltzed in, his hair dripping on his clean white T-
shirt, the water making little dark-colored blobs on his
shoulders. "I'm starved," he announced as he appropriated
a chair and plopped down. Ignoring both the neatly folded
napkin and his fork, he gestured to the plate in Marie's
hand and asked, "That mine?"

"Yes," Marie said as she put the top on the second sandwich. "Here you go."

Jason snatched the plate away from her and added two huge handfuls of chips. He bypassed the applesauce totally and picked up the first sandwich. Meat juice dripped down from the sandwich's sides and dribbled over his fingers as he opened his mouth wide in preparation for the first bite.

"Wait," Marie ordered as she glanced around the table.

Jason froze, staring at her over the top of his sandwich, mouth still open.

"What?" Luke asked, lowering his own fork.

Carolyn just blinked at her.

"We have to say grace."

Jason's face contorted into a mask of pain. "Man, I thought we were done with stupid stuff like that. You haven't gone off the deep end and insisted on grace in over a month. What is it with you?" He turned and spoke to Luke. "She's like a religious fanatic or something. Why, I remember this one time about a week or so after she first came back home we decided to have pizza. Naturally we couldn't order out. Oh, no, Marie the cheapskate has to cook her own. Swears it's better than carryout anyway." Jason rolled his eyes. "Yeah, right. Whatever. So she forgets to set the timer. The thing is all burned, I mean the cheese is practically black."

"It was not," Marie hotly defended. She pleaded her case directly to Luke. "It was just a little well-done, that's all. The cheese was sort of a, um, kind of a deep brown."

Jason snorted. "Black. It was black."

Marie crossed her arms over her chest. "Brown. Dark brown."

Jason ignored her. "So anyways, there we were having this lump of carbon for dinner and Marie makes us say grace over it. Can you believe it? Like I was grateful."

"There are starving children who would have been glad to have that pizza," Marie informed her uncle, not believing the words were coming out of her mouth even as they spilled out. She was turning old right before her own eyes. Next thing you knew, she'd be recollecting about how she remembered when candy bars were a dime...or worse, a nickel.

"And there was salad as I recall that had absolutely nothing wrong with it. And a bowl of cut-up fruit."

Jason circled a finger in the air. "Wow. A couple of lettuce leaves and a cut-up apple. Whoop-de-do."

"How much of that meal did you help create?" Luke asked Jason softly.

"What?"

"You heard me. How much of that meal did you get on the table yourself? Seems to me you had a lot to be grateful for. And we're not eating charcoal tonight, are we?"

Jason looked taken aback. "Well, no. This stuff's okay. I guess." Jason set his sandwich down and licked his fingers. "But I still don't see why we have to say grace," he quickly inserted lest his two adversaries think they'd won the war.

"I don't, either," Luke admitted, but before Jason had time to gloat, Luke continued. "But if Marie wants to say it, then we say it. You've got to learn to pick your battles, buddy. It won't kill either one of us to go along with the plan here."

Jason, who Marie had decided loved to argue just to argue, looked ready to jump back into the fray. "That's like so stupid—"

Marie nodded at Carolyn. "Jason, this is simple. Since the moment you were born Grandpa and Grandma Pearl harped on me about setting a good example for you. Now it's your turn to worry about the next generation turning out. With age comes responsibility. You're no longer the baby. When we have a little one over there visiting, you'll watch your mouth and we'll say grace when we eat. Deal with it."

"But—"

"Bless us, oh Lord—"

"Oh, man—"

"And these thy gifts—" Luke's deep baritone took up the prayer as he reached over and showed Carolyn how to fold her hands properly, then changed his mind and took one of her little hands in his. He reached over to take Marie's with the other.

Sighing gustily, Jason grabbed Marie's and Carolyn's remaining hands, completing the circle. "Which we are about to receive—" he reluctantly joined in for the third line.

Marie sat back with a sigh of relief once grace was successfully completed. She'd actually won a round. Of course, it hadn't hurt that Luke had backed her up. He hadn't understood her reasoning until she'd explained it, but he'd assumed there'd been some and went along with the program. There'd been no choice but for Jason to fall into line. Gosh, what a difference it made when there was someone with whom to present a united front.

She fixed her own plate. Taking the remaining half bun, Marie began to ladle the sloppy joe mixture over it. Her stomach roiled.

Darn, what was wrong with her? She served herself a scant spoonful, looked at the bowl of grease-stained potato chips and had to make a real effort not to gag. Whatever was wrong with her was not going to allow Marie to ignore it much longer, that was for sure. "Excuse me, will you?" she murmured, pushing her chair back.

Luke watched Marie all but flee the room. He turned to look at Jason. "What was that about?"

Jason shrugged. "I don't know. She probably wanted me to cut up my sloppy joe and eat it with a fork. But that takes too long, you know? I'd be dead of starvation with the food right in front of me. Or maybe I had my mouth open again while I chewed. That really grosses her out. But I swear I'm not that loud when I eat. You didn't notice

anything, did you? I mean, you should hear some of my
friends eat. They're real pigs,'' Jason told Luke. He stopped
his monologue just long enough to lick more meat juice
from between his fingers. ''Marie says nobody's going to
want to marry me if I don't learn to chew with my mouth
shut, but my friend Lloyd? Well, he's got a girlfriend and
you can hear him eat from a mile away. Of course his
girlfriend is a total dog. Like, this chick barks and everything. He was probably the only guy she could get, but
even still—''

Luke pushed his own chair back. ''Watch after Carolyn
for a minute, will you, Jason? Make sure she doesn't choke
or anything while I go check on Marie.''

''Dude, I'm telling you she's fine. I'm always grossing
her out. This is perfectly normal. Same thing happened at
breakfast just yesterday and I hadn't even started eating yet.
Hey, wait! Don't leave me here with the little peanut! I
don't know anything about—'' But Jason was speaking to
the breeze, all that was left to mark Luke's passing. ''Oh,
man,'' he moaned, then pointed a finger at Carolyn. ''Don't
you go choking on me, you hear me? I don't know what
to do if you choke. I don't even remember the dude's *name*
let alone how to do his maneuver thing.''

Jason ran his hand through his wet hair. ''Man, I hate to
say it, but Marie was maybe right. I should have paid more
attention when they made us learn that choking stuff. Here.
Give me that spoon. I'll feed you myself so I know you're
not putting too much in at one time. Now open up your
mouth and say 'ah.'''

''Ahhh.'' Carolyn thought Jason's game, whatever it
was, was pretty funny judging by the delighted look in her
eyes.

Jason carefully inspected her entire mouth right back to
her tonsils. ''Okay. Your mouth is empty.'' He shoveled
up a spoonful of applesauce and carefully fed it to her.
''Now chew that twenty times before you swallow. You've

got to be careful, you know," he lectured the tot. "Choking is, like, a major cause of death in little kids. At least I think I remember that dude-ette saying something like that." He watched her swallow then fed her the minutest bit of sloppy joe. "Okay now, remember. Twenty times." He waved an admonishing finger. "And don't you be letting me catch you running with hard candy in your mouth, you hear me? That stuff is lethal for young punks like you. Totally lethal. That I remember them saying for a fact in the health and families class I had to take, so you just watch it." Carolyn smiled angelically and swallowed.

"That wasn't twenty times. I know that wasn't twenty times." Jason was all but frantic. "Don't do this to me, kid. You want to die, you do it on your own time. I don't think I'd handle death very well, so you just behave yourself. If I say twenty, I mean twenty."

Luke would have laughed himself silly if he'd been able to hear Jason laying down the law to a two-year-old, but he had his hands full trying to locate his hostess. "Marie?" He stuck his head into the dining room. "You in here, Marie?"

He went on to the front parlor. "Marie?" This time he got a mumbled response.

"What?"

Luke entered the room and found her facedown on the sofa, her face buried in the seat cushion. "Hey, hey, what's the matter? I didn't think Jason's manners were all that bad. No worse than any other boy his age, I'd wager. Not enough to make you sick at any rate." Luke sat on the edge of the cushion beside her.

"It's not that," Marie mumbled into the cushion.

"Then what's wrong?" Luke asked, rubbing her shoulders and back gently.

"Something else."

Luke was nothing if not persistent. It was what made

him so good in the business world. "What kind of something else?"

Sighing, Marie turned her head toward him. Big mistake. Up close, he filled her vision as completely as his masculine scent filled her nose. Oddly enough, it did seem to make her stomach feel better. "Look, it has nothing to do with you, okay?"

Luke lightly shook her. "Listen, Marie, if you're getting sick you'd better let me know. Once I leave there won't be anybody here for you except Jason and somehow I don't see him feeding you chicken soup and soothing your fevered brow." Luke put the back of his hand to her forehead. "You don't feel hot."

Maybe not before he'd touched her, but she was hot now. His hand burned like a brand. "It's probably just a little virus," Marie prevaricated, wondering if she could wish it true.

"Jason says you couldn't eat your breakfast yesterday, either."

"Jason's got a big mouth," Marie muttered.

"He's worried about you."

Marie snorted. "Yeah, right."

Luke brushed the hair back off her forehead in an oddly gentle gesture for such a large man. "You weren't sick yesterday when we drove to Kalamazoo."

"No. No, I was fine by then."

"Were you up late the night before last?"

An odd sense of contentment combined with lethargy crept through Marie's body. Luke's body radiated heat, warming her. His masculine scent seemed the antidote for the smell of the sloppy joes. Her stomach was settling right down. Her eyelids were suddenly incredibly heavy and she was losing the battle to keep them open. "Hmm? No, as I recall I got to bed relatively early. Jason's friend, the one who had access to a car, was grounded so I didn't have to stay up and wait for Jason to get in. It was great."

"Yet you slept most of the way up to Kalamazoo."
Thoughtfully Luke tapped the fingers of one hand on his
thigh.

Marie's eyes popped open. "Yes. So?"

"Off again on again nausea, fatigue...Marie—"

"Luke, I think I know where you're going with this and
I don't like it."

She didn't like it? *She* didn't like it? Hadn't he already
been here, done this? What, Marie hadn't noticed the little
bundle of joy he'd left out there in the kitchen with her
uncle? Just what he needed. Another baby he had absolutely nothing to do with producing. Of course, she had no
way of knowing... "Just tell me if it's a possibility."

Marie sighed. Regretfully she sat up. "Maybe I'm in a
state of denial, but I just don't see how it's possible."

Luke pounced on her logic. "You wouldn't be in a state
of denial if it wasn't possible, would you?"

Again she sighed. "Look, you knew your brother and I
had separated."

Luke nodded. "I knew. But you were back together
when he had the accident."

"Yes, he'd called a few months ago. Wanted me back.
Promised he'd changed. No more other women. Even
agreed to go to a marriage counselor so we could work
things out." Marie raked her hand through her hair. "Oh,
heck. I don't want to speak ill of the dead and he was your
brother, after all."

Luke prodded. "Go ahead, I can handle it."

"The thing is, Wade wasn't exactly Mr. Maturity."

Wow, there was a news flash. He'd only grown up with
Wade. Who'd have thought?

"Neither was I when I married him. I mean, Grandpa
tried to warn me, but I—well, at the time I thought I was
in love. But the plain truth is, I didn't know the meaning
of the word. In retrospect, I was a late maturer although I
sure thought I was Mrs. Maturity at the time. I mixed up

an appreciation of physical perfection for love, okay? Initially, at least, I don't think I could see past Wade's biceps and I'm pretty sure he married me for my...never mind. You can guess. It was an unhappy discovery when I realized there wasn't much to our relationship beyond that, okay? Your brother was sort of stuck in an adolescent time warp or something. Drove too fast, drank too much. He point-blank refused counseling. Insisted I was the one with the problems. He was just fine. We were married, but he had several other women who agreed with him, too.''

Luke knew all those things. He'd assumed Marie had been involved, had at least turned a blind eye if she hadn't outright condoned or participated in his brother's vices. He looked at her blankly. ''Why in the world did you agree to go back?''

''I got married too young, but once it was done I took those vows seriously. Wade finally asked me to leave. Told me I was too conservative, that I cramped his style. Said my body was false advertising. I was so torn up after he asked me to leave I'd scheduled myself for breast reduction surgery. Wade almost had a heart attack when he called. He agreed to get counseling and I felt I had to give things another chance.'' She shrugged. ''So, I went back and we—'' she gave him an embarrassed glance ''—well, we, you know—got together. I mean, we were trying to reconcile, after all.''

Luke hung his hands between his knees and studied them. ''Yeah, I know. So what you're saying is it's more than possible that you're—'' He gestured to her stomach.

She gave him a disapproving look. ''I'm not totally stupid. It was an unstable situation, I knew that. I made him use a—you know.''

Luke nodded his understanding of the device in question.

''There was this one night—only one time, mind you, well, it broke.''

''It broke?'' Luke asked in disbelief.

Marie nodded solemnly. "I didn't know it at the time, but he was already cheating on me again. He missed our counseling session for the third time in a row a few days later and two days after that ran his car into a tree. Legally, he was drunk and there was a...a woman in the car with him. She wasn't badly hurt, more shaken up. Actually she came to the funeral to offer her condolences and tell me how lucky I was to have had a great guy like Wade who really knew how to have fun and how much she was going to miss good old Wade. Nice of her, huh?"

Luke had turned his head sideways to stare at her. "Good God."

"Yeah. So you see, I could be, but I just can't. I mean, one time?"

For a long time Luke just sat there, transfixed. Finally he spoke. "This is very heavy-duty."

"Tell me about it."

"Hey, you guys, where are you?" Jason's voice boomed from the kitchen. "Peanut woman is done with her dinner. Thanks a lot for deserting me, you two, but she's still alive, no thanks to either one of you. What do I do with her now?"

"Coming," Marie called and started to rise.

Luke planted a hand on her thigh, holding her in place. Marie looked over questioningly. "What?"

"I've got to think about this for a while."

Startled, she responded, "There's nothing for you to think about. It's my problem."

"Marie? Luke? I'm not staying out here all night with the little princess."

"How much milk did she drink?" Marie called.

"I don't know. Whatever was in the cup. An inch, maybe two."

"She needs more calcium than that. I made tapioca. It's loaded with milk. Give her some of that. It's there on the stove."

"How much do I give her?"

"Half a cup. A third of a cup. Whatever."

"Well, which is it? A third or a half? And where are the measuring cups?"

Marie began to lose her patience. "Jason, this isn't chemistry class. It doesn't have to be all that precise. Just put some in a plastic bowl and give it to her. Oh, stick your finger into it and make sure it's cooled down enough, first."

"Oh, man—"

"She said we'd be right there," Luke boomed. "Keep your pants on and cope if you want me to take you out driving."

"Jason wears his pants so big, that'll be a challenge. I can't figure out how he keeps them on at all. Force of habit is all I can come up with."

Luke looked at her disapprovingly. "This is not a joking matter."

"Oh, so what would you suggest? I should shoot myself? It's laugh or kill myself."

"Don't be ridiculous. First things first. We've got to get you tested."

Marie sniffed. "You make it sound like I might be rabid or something. Don't worry. You won't need shots. It's not catching. You're safe."

That's what she thought. If Marie was pregnant Luke figured he'd be caught good and proper. The good news was this baby would at least be related to him. Luke took his familial responsibilities seriously. There were times when he wished like hell he could be more like Wade and more or less go through life giving the world the finger, but no, falling right in with the typical psychological profile of family dynamics, as the oldest, he'd played the role of the responsible one.

"Marie, if you're...expecting—" he could hardly get the word out "—then you need to see about prenatal care. I'm pretty sure there are special vitamins for pregnant women and, I don't know…other things you should be doing to ensure the baby is born healthy.''

Marie stared at Luke. But if she got the test it would all become real. There'd be no more pretending.

Of course there was always the chance it could come back negative. It was possible.

Yeah, right. So if she wasn't pregnant, what was wrong with her? Leukemia? Now there was a happy alternative. At least if she was pregnant she'd eventually be okay again. Like in twenty-one years. Marie sighed. She'd better start taking care of herself, she supposed. Calcium. She needed calcium to insure her progeny's strong bones. "Let's go have some tapioca," she said and led the way back to the kitchen.

Chapter Five

Luke stayed long enough to see the kitchen cleaned. It was never too early to start teaching responsibility, he decided, so Carolyn was allowed to pull up a chair and stick her hands in the soapy water where she "helped" wash the dishes. Her job seemed to involve spreading soapsuds everywhere and soaking herself in the process. The washing process took longer but there were side benefits. For one, Luke figured he could probably skip Carolyn's bath that night. He also assigned Jason the task of clearing the table, barely catching him before he made his getaway good. There was a lot of groaning and complaining, but the job got done.

Luke took his leave as soon as the kitchen was back into shape. Carefully buckling Carolyn into her safety seat, Luke headed into a glorious pink-and-gold sunset and wound his way back home. He tucked his car into the garage, Carolyn into her new jammies and then Carolyn and her jammies into bed. He sat beside her and had to smile at the way she nestled into him while he reread for easily the twentieth time, or so it seemed, Dr. Seuss's *One Fish,*

Two Fish, Red Fish, Blue Fish, one of only three books all of a similar ilk that had come with Carolyn. At the end of the story Luke kissed her forehead, turned off the overhead light and plugged in the night-light he'd purchased. Making a mental note to stop in the children's section of the mall's biggest book store before bedtime tomorrow—surely the good doctor had written more than three books—he slipped out of Carolyn's room and down the stairs.

Luke rarely drank more than the occasional Monday night football beer but tonight he made straight for the liquor cabinet and poured himself a good stiff belt of whiskey. Drink in hand, Luke made his way into his study. He slipped some hard-core stuff into his state of the art CD player and dialed the volume low so as not to disturb Carolyn. Then he rounded the desk and sat in his padded leather chair. Slouching into the chair and pushing back, Luke put his feet up on the desktop and contemplated life, cosmic and personal.

"Crud." Which was not what he wanted to say. His personal preference had always been for a good, strong, four-letter Anglo-Saxon word, but even alone he was feeling pressed in and inhibited. What if his preferred word was to slip out in front of Carolyn? Potential playmates' mothers would refuse to let their progeny play with her. She'd be ostracized, friendless, all because he'd slipped up and inadvertently taught his daughter to swear. Luke vowed then and there to watch himself.

"Stink," he muttered, which didn't even have four letters, and took a healthy swig of whiskey. He liked the way it burned its way down into his belly, and took another.

For a long time, Luke sat in the dark, imagining the music was blasting his eardrums—there was something ludicrous about hard rock played at a whisper, wasn't there? It sort of negated the benefits of surround sound. Luke shrugged. Whatever. He sat there imagining the ear-piercing sounds of amplifiers on overload and contemplated his circumstances.

He wanted to throw something, but that would be immature and he'd only have to clean the mess he created, so the gestures would be sort of self-defeating. Then, too, Carolyn might cut her foot on whatever he smashed if he missed a shard. Marie's directive to Jason to be conscious of setting a good example in front of Carolyn had really struck home. It had been a while since he'd been to any type of Sunday service. Luke needed to look into what was available in his new neighborhood. He had no idea what kind of ranking his current school district had. Hell, he'd barely moved in, had in fact just gotten the stereo system properly installed and now he might have to consider relocating. After they stopped at the bookstore tomorrow he should run into one of the department stores and get some pajamas—at least some bottoms for himself. Carolyn didn't need *that* kind of education.

The list was endless. At home care or day care center? He'd taken a month's leave but that would rapidly slip by. There was a lot to consider and take care of before he went back to work. Carolyn was used to living with her mother. Would seeing his hairy chest psychologically scar her for life? Heck if he knew. Maybe he should get a full set of pajamas no matter how confining he found them.

And then there was Marie.

Good God in heaven above—and that was no prayer— as if he didn't have enough problems, there was Marie.

"The test will be positive," he decided as he sat there in the darkened room nursing his Scotch. "No doubt in my mind. Not the way my luck's been running. It'll be positive. Then what'll I do?"

Jason wasn't the problem. Marie might not understand him, but Luke didn't foresee any major problems there. Not only was Luke a former male adolescent himself but he was twice Jason's size and teenage boys responded well to intimidation. No, if push came to shove he could handle that part of things. It was Marie and her possible precious little burden that terrorized him. A two-year-old and a baby, neither one of them biologically his.

"What's fair about that?" he asked the darkness.

"Where's the justice?"

He could virtually hear his mother's response. *And whoever said life was fair?*

Sure, he'd been a baby and even a two-year-old himself once upon a time. Who hadn't? That didn't mean he remembered anything about it or gained any significant insight on how to handle the breed. It had been too long ago.

Marie, however, Luke reminded himself, was very good with little Carolyn. Of course, she was in over her head with her obnoxious uncle. Too bad they couldn't swap, Luke thought and finished off his Scotch.

Swap. Hmm. Luke shrugged. Nah, too complicated. And he hadn't even met the grandfather yet who was part of the package deal with Jason. Nah.

Luke stared down at the hand currently squeezing the empty whiskey glass.

He had a strong grip, a legacy of working out on a regular basis. His mother had always passed him the jars with recalcitrant lids and he'd usually won at arm wrestling.

"Except with Wade," he muttered, being scrupulously honest even with himself. Of course, Wade had taken steroids so he didn't really count. Looking down, Luke realized that the hand he was so engrossed in admiring was going to be cut to ribbons if he didn't stop strangling his glass. Luke loosened his grip until the whiteness of his knuckles eased.

She'd mentioned an initial attraction to Wade's biceps.

Damn it, Wade had always had women throwing themselves. It had been disgusting. No depth to his relationships at all. The women had only been interested in Wade's body.

He'd been jealous as hell.

Luke let his eyes move up his forearm. He squinted, trying to see it through a female perspective as if that was possible. The female brain was an enigma to beat all enigmas. But honest to God, try as he might he couldn't see anything wrong with his forearm, either. "It's a damn decent forearm," he told himself and wondered if he mightn't be getting just the slightest bit drunk. His arm's topside was lightly furred with a silky coating of neat black hair.

"Not exactly King Kong," he muttered to himself, "but who wants King Kong? As I recall, the women all ran in the opposite direction."

What in holy hell had been so special about Wade's biceps?

Luke let go of the glass altogether and held his arm out in front of himself. He studied his upper arm. He flexed and studied it some more.

"There's not a darn thing wrong with my biceps," he informed the darkness. "And my triceps are nothing to sneeze at, either," he announced after a thorough examination and *knew* he'd had too much to drink. Still he couldn't stop his analysis.

"Okay, I like being able to button my shirts around my neck so I don't take steroids. Big deal. I work out. I'm as buff as the next guy. A lot buffer than some." Luke had been in enough locker rooms to know. He was over six feet. His shoulders were broader than most. His hips tapered, damn it all. So how come, at least lately, his greatest appeal seemed to be among the two-year-old set? Maybe he'd been too involved in his work. That must be it. Luke flexed harder.

"Look, my veins stand out, too. So how come nobody's ever thrown themselves at *me* for my biceps?"

Luke stared at his empty glass. Since when had one whiskey been too much? Oh, he was being pathetic, all right. Surely he'd have been turned off and dismayed by anyone pursuing him strictly for his body. How shallow. How surface.

Surely he would not have succumbed. Surely not.

"But it would be nice to inform them I was above that kind of thing."

Disgusted, Luke hauled himself out of his chair and put himself to bed.

Things would look better in the morning.

"They'll have to. They certainly couldn't look any worse."

Carolyn came in and bounced on the bed at five-thirty the next morning.

"Daddy, Daddy, gotta go potty. Daddy, Daddy, I gotta—"

Luke stirred groggily. "Wha—who?" He did his best to open his eyes but met with only minimal success. "Carolyn, honey, sweetheart, is that you?"

"Gotta go potty. *Now,* Daddy."

Luke was finally able to focus. Sort of. Judging by the way Carolyn was fidgeting and jumping around, the little tike wasn't kidding around. Luke's eyes widened in alarm and he threw the sheets back. He scooped up the child like a football and ran for the goal post; in this case, the bathroom. He'd spent this month's bonus on refurbishing the bedroom for Carolyn. He wasn't prepared to replace his bedroom carpeting as well. Luke breathed a sigh of relief when he was at least over the ceramic tiles of the bathroom. Setting her down, he quickly wrestled open the snaps that held Carolyn's bottoms up to the tops of her little sleeper then he boosted her up onto the toilet.

Man, who'd have thought he could move so fast this early in the morning?

"There you go, sweet cheeks. We made it."

Luke knew his life had hit an all-time low when he cheered the sound of his new daughter's success in the bathroom. "Good girl, cupcake. That's the way. What a big girl you are."

His heart slowed back down about the same time he was done putting Carolyn back together after their close call. "That was a close one, huh, sweetie?"

"You so funny, Daddy."

"I'm glad you think so, pumpkin. It's nice that one of us is finding life entertaining just now."

"I get a tweat?"

Luke was getting good at interpreting two-year-oldese. "A treat? At this time of the morning? What for?"

"I stay dwy all night long. I a good girl."

Luke carried Carolyn down the hall while dubiously eyeing her. Evidently this was something of an accomplishment for her. Perhaps he should put some kind of mattress protector on his shopping list. Did they still make rubber sheets? He remembered them from his childhood. Not personally, of course, but he recalled Wade having to have one on his bed until he was around eight.

Luke smiled evilly and wondered what Marie would think if he casually let *that* out of the bag. She'd been such a sucker for the guy's biceps. Well, how about his kidney and bladder? Huh? What about those? They hadn't been so hot, now had they?

Luke collapsed back on his bed, Carolyn still in his arms. The tot giggled and snuggled in close. Luke lay there, Carolyn's head on his shoulder. Luke sighed. Well, there he was in bed with a clinging woman. Somehow the reality was not quite up to the mental imagery, but you know what? It wasn't half bad, either. He hugged the tot and pulled the sheets up. It was too damn early to get up. Hell, the sky was barely beginning to gray. You couldn't even call it dawn. Surely he could coax Carolyn into closing her eyes and conking out for another hour or two.

Half an hour later Luke gave up. Carolyn was wide-awake and in between bouts of thoughtful thumb sucking and chattering as enthusiastically as whatever kind of bird was outside his window that needed strangling. What the heck was wrong with its mate or kids or whoever it was calling to?

"What are they, deaf? Man, if and when I ever get married, if my wife nags at me like that bird then I'm gone. History, I tell you." It would be different if Marie was in the bed with him. The bird could sing until it went hoarse and Luke would only cheer it on. Marie could nag and it wouldn't bother him at all. The world would be a better, brighter place with Marie in his arms. The nights would do a lot for brightening up the days.

Luke began to secretly fear he was as shallow as his brother.

Carolyn leaned her little head back over his arm and peered up at him. "What you saying, Daddy?"

Luke looked down and wondered how the tot could focus at such a short distance. His own eyes were all but crossing. "I'm saying we ought to get up and face the new day. It appears to be here ready or not."

"You put on Ariel, Daddy?" Carolyn requested, somehow recognizing Luke's speech as recognition that it was okay to start moving. She turned onto hands and knees and began bouncing on the bed. "Ariel! Ariel!" she chanted.

Personally Luke would rather kill himself. Desperately he cast about for an alternative. "Well, now first let's go down to the kitchen and see about breakfast. It's not good to watch television during meal times, you know, sweetheart. Gospel truth. Families are supposed to use that time to talk to each other and, uh, bond or something like that."

"Ariel! Ariel!"

Luke sat up, brushed his hair back out of his face and stood. Thank God he'd thrown on an old pair of sweat pants before he'd crawled into bed. Reaching out an arm, Luke snagged Carolyn around her waist and tucked her in close to his body. He carried her down to breakfast as if she were an oversize football.

He poured Carolyn a mound of vitamin fortified something or other and gave her half an inch of milk in the bottom of a glass.

"Gotta get one of those cups with a sipping lid," he muttered. "I'm already tired of mopping up spilled juice."

It was his last conversational gambit. He put on the coffeemaker and sat and siphoned in caffeine while he stared at Carolyn. It was six-forty five in the damn morning.

"Gonna be a long day," he finally sighed.

"Ariel!"

It didn't make him happy, but he needed help. He perceived it as a weakness. Luke reached for the phone anyway. He was a desperate man.

"Marie? It's Luke here," he said at the sound of her voice. She was wide-awake at this hour. She'd mentioned yesterday how she liked to get up early and she wasn't kidding apparently. "I was wondering what you had planned for the day."

Going to a nursing home. Wonderful. Well, it beat anything on his own agenda. "That's too bad your grandfather is having trouble with the staff there. Did you check out the place's credentials? What home is it?

"Really? Maybe I ought to come along with you. I have an aunt who works there. In fact, I think she works days. She'll probably be on by the time we get there. She'll know who to talk to, how to get things straightened out."

Luke finished his coffee, ran the kitchen tap to rinse the mug and set it in the sink. "How about if I pick you up in an hour?"

It was doubtful he'd last that long, but he supposed eight o'clock was a more civilized time to go visiting. And he definitely preferred helping to being helped. "All right. Eight o'clock it is. See you then." He hung up the phone.

Luke cleaned up the breakfast mess.

That took all of ten minutes.

He put on the television for Carolyn and found the PBS station. Luke had a feeling he'd soon have their schedule by heart. An early morning broadcast of *Sesame Street* was on, praise the Lord. He'd heard of that show. Kids liked that, didn't they? He rubbed a finger along the side of his nose while he checked out the first few minutes with Carolyn. She was already mesmerized but Luke wasn't sure that a giant yellow bird was all that preferable to a woman with green scales and a flipper for legs. Good grief, what was that thing? The canary that ate the world? Sighing, he left the room to go get dressed. It was time to officially face the day with a shower and a shave. He was brave. He was strong. He could handle it.

He was a coward. He was a wuss. And he would probably kill himself by noon. Those were the thoughts passing through Luke's mind as he steered his rental car over to Marie's an hour and a half later. It was a quarter to eight in the morning and big, brave, strong Luke Deforest needed a nap. A two-year-old had worn him out. It was humiliating. Young children should come with power switches. Turn them on for an hour or two each day for a bit of the "quality time" psychologists were always harping about and the rest of the time you kept them in some sort of suspended animation so you could conserve energy for the next bout of required "quality time."

Luke pulled into Marie's driveway and shut off the engine. He retrieved Carolyn from her car seat and marched up to the front door scowling. "Out of the frying pan and into the fire," he muttered under his breath as he heard Marie's footsteps. Luke felt his lower body stir to life just from the *sound* of her walking. His imagination supplied the rest. He could see the gentle sway of her hips in his mind's eye. He could even already smell the hint of raspberry from whatever shampoo she used. Had he no sense? How could he let his body overrule his common sense like this? He shouldn't be here. Marie was trouble, pure and simple. She had *complication* written all over her and it just didn't matter. Luke wanted her, damn it, and he didn't like that little fact at all.

"Hi," Marie said as she opened the door. Her eyes widened when she noticed his black scowl. "What's the matter?"

Besides the fact that his entire life was in the toilet? "Nothing. It's just been a long morning, that's all."

Marie looked at him blankly. "It's not even nine o'clock yet."

"Feels like the middle of the afternoon," he muttered as he ran one hand through his hair and used the other to usher Carolyn into the house. "She's been up since five-thirty."

"You're lucky she's a morning person," Carolyn said and Luke gave her a look that said she'd lost her mind.

"No, seriously. It's only the second week of school and you would not believe the trouble I had getting Jason up and out the door this morning. World War III just about broke out, I'm telling you. I mean, I had nothing to do with scheduling his classes. It's not my fault sophomore English has to study Shakespeare's *Merchant of Venice* and his teachers are all jerks, is it? He's still got to go."

Luke grunted. He didn't feel remotely sorry for her. "Getting to school on time is Jason's responsibility, not yours, Marie. Tell him to set his own alarm and then ignore him in the morning. He'll be late a couple of times but a few bouts of Saturday school will quickly cure that. Don't let him pull you into conflicts that aren't yours."

Marie simply stared at him, awestruck. "You know what? That's a great idea. Why didn't I think of that? Hmm, make him take responsibility for himself. It's certainly about time. He's almost sixteen for heaven's sake. Thank you, Luke."

Luke grunted and waved away her thanks. "Getting Jason out of the house is a piece of cake compared to what I went through this morning."

"Oh, yeah?"

"Yeah." He gestured at Carolyn who was calmly standing there sucking her thumb. "For one thing, she came this close—" he held up his thumb and forefinger so they were practically touching "—this close to ruining all my upstairs carpeting."

Suddenly Marie was all concern. She dropped to her knees and hugged Carolyn. "What's the matter, Caro, did you get sick? How's your tummy now, darling?"

Luke rolled his eyes. "No, she's not sick. She must have drunk too much before she went to bed. She glugged down almost an entire cup of water when she brushed her teeth. How much salt do you think was in that sloppy joe stuff? She was really thirsty. Anyway, her little kidneys were working overtime filtering out impurities during the night and her bladder sensor didn't go off until it was almost too late. You know anyplace that sells rubber sheets? I'm thinking I ought to protect the mattress and the carpet somehow. Maybe lay down a roll of plastic stripping from her bed to the bathroom."

It was Marie's turn to roll her eyes. "You're being ridiculous."

Luke was highly insulted. "I am not. Decent carpeting costs, you know."

She nodded her head. "I know, I know, but you're overreacting. Just don't let her drink an entire glass of water right before bedtime. Did you make sure she went to the bathroom before she lay down?"

Luke tried to remember. He'd been a lot more interested in figuring out how to snap the little jammies together. "Uh—"

"Why don't you try limiting her intake of fluids in the evening?"

Damn if that wasn't a good idea. Luke was coming to

the unhappy conclusion that he and Marie would make a good team. He'd have had no problem kicking Jason's butt out the door in time for class this morning and Marie could have dealt far better with little Caroline, he was sure. It angered Luke that he'd already sunk to using the television as baby-sitter so early in the game. It did not bode well for further down the road.

"I'll try that tonight," he said gruffly, leaving Marie to assume he wasn't grateful at all for the suggestion when the exact opposite was true.

"Okay. Fine. Good. You ready to go?"

Luke stared at her blankly. "Go— Oh, yeah. The nursing home. Yeah. I guess."

"Look, you don't have to come. I can deal with this by myself. You and Carolyn could stay here and wait for me."

"No!" Luke shouted his denial of being left on his own again. He modulated his tone when Carolyn jumped in response. "I mean, that's all right. We don't mind coming along. It's supposed to be good for little kids to interact with seniors. Today's nuclear families deny children the wisdom, experience and loving their grandparents lavished on them in a less mobile society, as well as the support and baby-sitting parents used to count on." He had no idea if that was true or not but it sounded good and Luke was not going to be left behind and alone with Carolyn so long as there was a viable alternative available.

"And besides," he continued, thinking fast, "it might be better if you tell me exactly what your grandfather's objecting to and let me do the talking. Sometimes these places take complaints from a man more seriously than from a woman."

Marie immediately opened her mouth to object and Luke held up a hand. "I'm not saying it's right for them to do that, just that it happens."

And because Luke seemed to want them to be on their way, Marie very quickly found herself riding shotgun in

Luke's car as he efficiently backed down the drive and smoothly accelerated down the street. "Nice car," she said for lack of anything more scintillating to bring up.

"It's a dark blue four-door sedan," Luke returned. "How exciting is that?"

Marie was immediately defensive. She could read between the lines. He was insinuating that it was her fault he was driving this boring car. "The upholstery's...plush," she returned. What was it about Luke that consistently put her back up?

"Never mind pitching me the car," Luke said. "It's gone the moment mine is ready to be picked up. Instead, tell me exactly what's going on with your grandfather. You don't think we're talking elder abuse, do you?"

"If I thought that he'd already be out of there ready or not."

Luke grunted. "Right. Sorry. So what do you think is up?"

"This is new. The first time he mentioned it was last night on the phone. His complaints all seem to center around this one aide. She's brusque and abrasive from what I can tell. At any rate they certainly seem to rub each other the wrong way. Maybe your aunt knows her and can help me figure out a way to keep her away from Grandpa. I don't know, trade duties with this witch or something."

Luke considered that as he steered around a parked car. "It's a possibility. But that leaves some other poor slob at the tender mercies of this witch. Maybe they ought to just can her ass."

Marie checked over the seat back. Carolyn was being mesmerized by the hypnotic movement of the automobile and was half asleep. "Shh, not in front of the baby."

Luke had to stop himself from smacking his own forehead. "Right. Sorry, I forgot."

"Well, you can't forget anymore. Think before you open your mouth."

"I said I was sorry."

He sounded as petulant as Jason. Marie rolled her eyes and remained silent the rest of the way to the nursing home.

"Grandpa? Hi, how are you feeling this morning?"

Marie's grandfather looked up from his bed and beamed. "Well, well, look who's here. And I was just thinking how that little patch of overcast sky I can see out of that excuse for a window matched my mood and who waltzes in the door? My own ray of sunlight. Come give your wretched, old, feeling-sorry-for-himself granddad a kiss, sweetheart, and tell me what you're doing out so early in the morning."

Marie left the doorway and ran across the linoleum tiled floor to her grandfather's bed. Carefully she wrapped her arms around him and squeezed while she kissed his cheek. "You're feeling better, aren't you? You've got a little color back."

"I'm not quite ready to dance at anyone's wedding, but yes. Except for when they torture me during what they laughingly call physical therapy I don't hurt nearly so much." Marie's grandfather patted her hand. "Honey, next time you come I want you to bring me the bills for this place. I want to see what they're charging for that physical therapy stuff. I'll bet it's a damn fortune. Then I think I'll call around and compare what they do and how much we're getting hosed, with some of the other facilities in town."

"Now don't go getting yourself all worked up, Grandpa. You up and have a stroke because you put your blood pressure through the roof stewing and all you'll accomplish is lengthening your stay here. You know Dr. Mackley said this was the best place for you to be while you're recovering."

Her grandfather still gripped her hand. "I've decided the man's a quack. No other explanation. The things they do to you around here under the name of recovery aren't normal. And that aide I was telling you about?"

Marie stiffened. "What about her?"

"Direct descendant of the Marquis de Sade." Marie's grandfather nodded wisely. "I'm serious. Can't be any other explanation. Woman's a sadist. Thought they'd have to call the paramedics again just to get me back in here from the therapy room. And then they've got the nerve to charge for that medievalism they call therapy."

Luke was right, Marie decided. This woman, whoever she was, was going down. She would personally see to it that the wench was fired. Nobody picked on her grandfather and got away with it. It was nothing short of disgraceful to pick on somebody when they were weak. "That's why I'm here, Grandpa."

Luke cleared his throat.

Marie glanced over. He was standing just inside the doorway, a sleepy Carolyn in his arms waiting for an introduction, no doubt.

"Oh, sorry. Come on over, Luke. Grandpa, you'll remember Luke Deforest. He's Wade's older brother. You met him briefly at the wedding? Jason and I, um, sort of ran into him a couple of days ago and he stopped by the house. We're, uh, renewing our old acquaintance."

Her grandfather studied Luke from shrewd eyes. "That right?"

"Yes, that's right." Marie drew Luke and his daughter forward. "And this little sweetheart is Luke's daughter, Carolyn. She's just come to live with him. Her mother recently died. Remind you of anybody else you know, Grandpa?"

"Kids adjust quickly, Marie, you know that better than anybody else. She's a lot younger than you were and that'll make it easier." Her grandfather held up a hand. "But yes, I agree. It's a hard thing to have happen at any age."

"Luke, weddings are always confusing, so I'll introduce you once again to my grandfather, Ray Fort."

Luke stepped forward and, easily supporting Carolyn

with one brawny arm, offered a hand to the older man. He had sensed disapproval the minute Marie's grandfather had realized who Luke was and found himself relieved when his hand was accepted and firmly shaken without a male-territory-claiming hard squeeze.

"Mr. Fort, good seeing you again, sir."

"If you don't mind, I think I'll reserve judgment on that."

"Grandpa!"

"Sorry, sweetie," her grandfather apologized, as he winced and adjusted his position in the bed, "but the man's brother didn't take good care of my baby. He hurt you."

"Wade might have been clueless as to what a marriage was supposed to be all about but he never hit me, Grandpa," Marie lectured severely. "You know that."

"Hurt you in places where it doesn't show. Your mind, your feelings. Don't tell me it didn't take you a month of Sundays to recover from that fiasco of a marriage. I know better. I was there. And you can't expect me to welcome this one with open arms until I figure out if it was just the one apple gone bad or a problem with the entire barrel."

"You're being ridiculous," Marie sputtered.

"No, he's not," Luke contradicted. "I don't have to like it, but I do understand."

Ray Fort just shrugged, seemingly not caring whether the enemy understood or not so long as he was aware he was being watched and no funny business would be tolerated. "We'll see" was all her grandfather said.

Luke grudgingly admitted to himself that he liked the old guy. Despite his severe physical disadvantage, Marie's grandfather refused to give even an inch. The old guy called it like he saw it. A man had to respect that.

"So," her grandfather said. "I've got about fifteen minutes before reentering hell. Tell me how you and Jason are getting along."

"Fine, Grandpa. No problems. Jason and I are just like

this." Marie held up a hand with her middle finger crossed over the adjacent pointer to show the closeness existing between her uncle and herself.

Luke gave her a disbelieving look. "He's giving her fits," he stated.

Marie glared. "What'd you have to go and say that for? I don't want my grandfather worrying when he should be concentrating on getting well, for crying out loud."

Luke returned tit for tat. "Look at you, all pale and drawn looking. Like your grandfather isn't going to know something's wrong somewhere. He broke his hip, not his head. He's not stupid, you know."

"Of course he's not stupid. I just don't see what—"

"All right now. That's enough. Both of you stop. All this ruckus in a convalescent center. Get me kicked right out of here, which now that I think about it mightn't be too bad an idea at that. Probably recover one hell of a lot better at home," Mr. Fort grumbled and proceeded to nestle his head more comfortably back into his pillow as the room quieted down. "Marie, your young man's right. I know Jason. I'd be amazed if he wasn't giving you fits. I know you've been covering up. Hate to be beholden to a Deforest but I appreciate finally having this out in the open. Wasn't up to it before, but I am now. Let's talk about it. Strategize, if you will."

A large-boned sturdy-looking woman of indeterminate age swung through the doorway. She was handsome in a strong featured sort of way, her black hair with a good half inch of gray root showing pinned back off her face with a myriad of brown bobby pins, and snapping brown eyes. With her immense bosom and solid muscular build, she radiated energy and strength of purpose.

"Time to practice walking and stretch out those muscles again so they don't atrophy, Ray."

"Over my dead body," Marie's grandfather growled. "And that's Mr. Fort to you." He turned his attention to

Marie and whispered loud enough for everyone to hear. "That's the one. Evidently been on a different floor up until now. I want you to get me a book of names and their roots. She says her name is Betty. My guess is the name Betty is an Americanization of something along the lines of Bruen-hilde. See if I'm not right."

"Now, now—"

Marie took a deep breath and turned to face the dragon. "Perhaps it might be better if you and I stepped—" she began, then stopped dead when she heard Luke say,

"Hello, Aunt Bet."

Chapter Six

Marie turned to Luke, her eyes wide, her expression stunned. "*This* is your aunt? The dragon is your relative?" Marie threw up her hands. "Well, that's just great, isn't it? Fat lot of help you'll be now. You were going to help me get her rear fired, remember? We weren't going to stand for this. We were on a crusade, a mission from God and what happens? The playground bully turns out to be your aunt. Your aunt, for God's sake! You've probably already defected, haven't you? Well, that's just fine. That's just dandy. I can take care of my grandfather all by myself, just see if I can't." Marie turned toward the bed. "At least now we've got the answer to your question, Grandpa. It's the entire barrel."

"Marie," Luke began firmly, "just calm down. You're getting hysterical."

"Don't you tell me I'm getting hysterical, you turncoat. I'm not hysterical. Why, I've never been hysterical a day in my life. Jason should have hit your car harder. I should have put my foot over his on the accelerator."

Luke figured Marie would probably not respond well if

he told her to sit down and shut up. Women required a
more delicate touch. Luke tried again. Honest to God, the
woman could really roll when she got going. "Take a deep
breath, that's it. This can't be good for the ba—for your
blood pressure." Luke shot a quick look at Mr. Fort to see
if he'd noticed his slip but the old gent's arms were folded
over his middle while he sat back and obviously enjoyed
his granddaughter leaping to his defense and lambasting the
enemy.

"I just wish you'd shown this much spunk with that
bicep brain you were married to" was his only comment
and Luke knew there'd be no help forthcoming from that
quarter. Luke rolled his eyes ceilingward and threw up his
hands.

"Marie, that's your name, honey?" Luke's Aunt Betty
said, stepping forward. "I think you had the right of it.
Why don't you and I step into the hall for a minute? We'll
talk." Very gently for a woman who only needed steel
breastplates to enter an Attila the Hun's wife look-alike
contest, Betty took Marie's arm and drew her out into the
hallway. "We'll be right back, gentlemen. Luke, I don't
know what you're doing here, but good to see you. Ray,
don't go anywhere."

"Ha ha."

"That's it," Betty said, sounding almost fond. "Don't
lose that sense of humor. A good laugh can see you through
a lot."

Luke and Ray Fort eyed each other in silence for a minute or two.

Finally Luke cleared his throat. "That's quite a temper
your granddaughter's got. Don't know her all that well yet
but I have to admit that took me by surprise."

Ray nodded thoughtfully now that the show was over.
"Yes. If Marie's got a fault, it's that she's *too* understanding. Lets people walk on her, bottles it all up inside. Had
an insecure childhood, you know. Her dad walked out, then

her mother died. Came to live with us and her grandmother died. Marie had to adjust when I remarried and readjust when Jason came on the scene. Then my second wife died and once again there was no mother figure.'' Ray shook his shaggy head. ''No, she doesn't blow often...and this, it was different. Marie wasn't just mad. There was something else going on.''

And Luke knew what that something was. Pregnancy hormones. He'd heard about them. You didn't mess with a woman when she thought she was protecting her family and high as a kite on hormones. He grimaced as he thought of the mayhem he'd glimpsed in Marie's eyes and the un-called-for threats she'd made against his poor defenseless vehicle. That hurt. It had been a close call, all right.

''Down, Daddy,'' Carolyn said suddenly, piping up from her perch in Luke's arms.

''What? Oh sure, sweetie. Don't touch anything.''

Carolyn's thumb was in her mouth and she stood backed up snugly against Luke's leg for a moment or two before cautiously venturing forward to investigate the imposing hospital bed.

''Well, aren't you as pretty as a picture,'' Ray said as Carolyn edged closer. ''I don't like to credit your daddy's family with much but I have to admit that at least the gene for good looks is working. Where'd you get those big brown eyes? Not from Daddy, that's for sure. His eyes are blue. Mommy must have had brown eyes, huh?''

Luke froze. Maureen's eyes had been blue just like Luke's. Blue was a recessive gene. Any mythical child they'd have had together would have had blue eyes, no ifs ands or buts about it. Carolyn's warm chocolate-colored eyes had come from her biological father and that sure as shooting wasn't Luke. Luke had never touched Maureen. No, all he'd done was feel sorry for her which would certainly teach him the follies of compassion. By God, he was going to learn to harden himself against a woman's tears.

There was absolutely no excuse for the way he caved every time a woman's tear ducts went into overdrive. Just look at this current mess he was in. "Yes," Luke said casually, "her eyes are definitely from the other side of the family." A side so remote no one even knew about it...including that other side.

Ray seemed to accept that without question. "Like my bed, do you?" he asked.

Carolyn continued to suck and stare.

"Want to go for a ride on it?"

Carolyn appeared to think about it for a minute, glanced back at Luke, then held up her arms to Ray.

Ray looked frustrated, then glanced apologetically at Luke. "Give her a boost, will you?" he asked. "I can't lift her just yet."

Luke picked up his daughter beneath her arms and deposited her gently on the bed. "It won't be long now," he told Ray. "You're on the upswing."

Ray absently petted Carolyn's bright curls. "Taking too darn long. Worries me. I'm the only constant Marie's ever had and I'm getting old. Not bouncing back the way I used to."

"And you're scared," Luke said to himself with sudden insight. Then he directed a question to Ray. "Is that what this is all about with my aunt? You're frustrated and scared that things will never be the same? That somehow you're letting Marie and Jason down with your slower recovery? Are you worried about becoming a burden?"

Ray stared at him. "Never thought about it quite like that, but there might be a grain of truth in there somewhere." Ray shifted in his bed. "And I'm not scared. Worried, maybe, but not scared. And there's no *become* about it. Already am a darn burden."

Luke could almost feel the shackles tightening. Who did he think he was, he asked himself, Saint George? And how was it that every stinking person he met lately had some kind of damn dragon breathing fire down his or her back in desperate need of slaying? Luke was not a touchy-feely kind of guy but he managed to awkwardly pat the older man on the shoulder and say encouragingly, "Don't worry so much, Ray, things have a way of working out. You'll see." And he was very much afraid he knew how things were going to work themselves out. Saint George, aka Luke the martyr would shortly have yet another new cause—yet another in a long series of dragons that apparently needed killing.

"Listen, Ray, what's really happening here with my Aunt Betty? Obviously I've known her all my life and I've never known her to be mean or cruel. Firm, yes. I can see where the woman would run a tight ship but I simply can't believe she'd enjoy causing you pain."

Ray sighed as he began to work the bed controls, making the top of the mattress go up and down. He used his free arm to secure Carolyn and smiled gently when the toddler laughed out loud as she went for a ride. "Darn therapy hurts," he muttered. "Hurts a lot and I'm not all that convinced it's doing any good. Look at me, weeks later still trapped in this damn bed. And your aunt, she's so blasted cheerful all the time. Does she have to be so darn *happy* while she's torturing me? Almost like the woman enjoys seeing me in pain or likes lording it over me that she's the one in control. Your aunt's so, so—never mind. I hate being so darn helpless in front of her. You have no idea how much I hate it."

The light dawned. "My God. You're attracted to her, aren't you, you old goat? Already been through two wives and you've got your eye on another woman. Da...darn. That's incredible. I want to be just like you when I grow up. Ray, you're amazing."

"Don't be ridiculous. The woman's a witch. Ah, just exactly how old is your aunt, Luke?"

"Oh yeah, right. You're not interested. Pull the other one."

"Damn it, boy I'm not dead yet. And I'd have to be to not be interested. What's not to be interested in? Fine-looking woman. May end up killing myself getting my fill of a body like that. But I'd die with a smile on my face, guaranteed." Ray slapped the bed rails in emphasis.

Luke's eyes about bugged right out of his head. "Be careful what subjects you bring up in front of Carolyn." It was all he could think to say. Good Lord. Marie's *grandfather* was turned on by his *aunt*. The world as he knew it was coming to an end. Where was Chicken Little when you needed him? Someone had to spread the word. The sky was definitely in danger of falling. But he knew what the old man meant. He knew what it was like to be fixated on a particular woman's anatomy.

Still, he couldn't help but admonish the old guy. "Ray, that's my aunt you're talking about. I'll have you show a little respect."

Ray assumed a pious expression. "Believe me, son, I've got nothing but respect for Betty's physique."

This was insane. This was ridiculous. Why, Marie's grandfather was a dirty old man lusting after his virtuous aunt. Just thinking about it made his hair curl.

Luke took a quick glance in the mirror and patted his hair down flat.

Ray gave a sigh rich in melancholy. "But never mind that. I guess it's not important."

Not important? Luke was still reeling as though he'd taken a blow in the gut and it wasn't important?

"Nothing can come of it. Too old now, more's the pity. Lately I'm surprised every time I look in the mirror. Who is that old man looking back at me, I ask myself." Ray sighed. "Ah, well, time passes and you can't wish it back. Your aunt is safe from me. Now tell me what Marie meant when she said Jason hit you. What the heck happened?"

"Ah, nothing for you to worry about, Ray. A little one on one between your car and mine. Marie and I are handling it. I think she wants you concentrating on getting better."

"Oh, stow that." Ray shifted irritably then anchored Carolyn more securely when she began to slide. "It's not my mind that's broken, just my body. Tell me what happened."

"I think you should ask Marie."

"I'm asking you."

Luke studied the old man's face. There was strength there. Ray Fort had no doubt been a force to reckon with in his prime. There was still a lot of prime left, Luke decided, whether Ray realized it or not. Marie was naturally protective of her grandfather, but Luke wondered if she was giving the old gent enough credit. Ray needed something to chew on other than his own infirmity. Luke wondered, in fact, if Ray might not recover more quickly if he had a reason to get back on his feet. Ray talked about Marie needing him, but did he believe it?

"I ran into Marie, or should I say your son ran into me in the mall parking lot on Saturday." And Luke filled Marie's grandfather in on the weekend's happenings. After some brief consideration, he included Marie's here-again-gone-again nausea. The possibility of a great-grandchild ought to get Ray's ticker revved up once more, Luke decided.

"Well, damn."

Luke nodded his agreement of the assessment. "Yes, but Marie says we have to start watching our language in front of the wee one." Luke nodded significantly toward Carolyn. Luke was pleased with how comfortable Carolyn and Marie's grandfather were with each other. The old man was smiling softly and had his cheek resting on the top of Carolyn's soft curls. Carolyn was clinging to his broad chest and giggling happily.

"Yeah, she's probably right. Can't have a sweetheart like this swearing like a sailor."

When Marie walked back into her grandfather's room, Carolyn was nestled up against the old man's chest while he worked the hospital bed's control. The two of them were laughing like loons while Luke stood near the bed grinning.

Marie had to stop and stare. She'd never seen Luke smile like that. His teeth were even and white, his eyes were crinkled in the corners. He was gorgeous. Pulling her eyes away from him she was again dumbfounded by the child-like glee her grandfather displayed. When was the last time she'd seen him simply horse around and play like that? And Carolyn, well she was having the time of her life.

All those smiles directed at her made her nervous. "What's going on?"

"Not a blessed thing," her grandfather said, beaming at her with a smile Marie didn't trust an inch.

"Luke?"

Luke made a gesture of ignorance. "You heard your grandfather. Just giving Carolyn a ride, that's all. Why does anything have to be going on?"

"Because you look like the Cheshire Cat, that's why." Marie made a frustrated gesture. "Oh, never mind. Grandpa, I've been talking to Betty and she says—"

Her grandfather put up his hand in a stopping gesture. "I know, I know. It's got to be done. I still say the woman would be right at home in the Spanish Inquisition. She enjoys her work a little too much, but I'll go. Mind you, I'm still going to complain, but I'll cooperate."

Betty stuck her head into the door opening and beamed. "That's the spirit, Ray."

Ray rolled his eyes. "One of these days, Betty, one of these days. Fair warning. I won't always be crippled." Then, addressing Carolyn he said, "Time to get down, pumpkin. Grandpa Ray's got to go to the torture chamber. You come back and see me, all right?"

Marie eyed her grandfather uncertainly. "I can stay if you want, Grandpa."

Luke made a negative motion with his hand.

"No, no. You go ahead. Make sure the insurance forms are all properly filled out for Jason's accident. My rates will probably skyrocket. You might want to warn Jason that once I'm out of here he's going to be doing a lot of jobs around the house to work this one off. Don't just stand there, Betty, let's go. I've got to get out of here. I'm needed at home."

"Grandpa, I don't know what Luke's been telling you but I can handle things—"

Luke nudged her in the ribs. Marie gave him a puzzled look. "What?"

"Later," Luke said out of the side of his mouth.

They watched as Betty maneuvered Marie's grandfather out of the bed and into a wheelchair, waving as he was steered away.

"Now, what was that all about?" she asked as she took Carolyn's hand and they headed for the elevator.

"Your grandfather's a proud man," Luke told her.

"Well, of course he is. And with every justification."

"He doesn't like you seeing him helpless or being perceived as helpless. He doesn't even want Betty, a virtual stranger, seeing him like this."

"Why ever not?" Marie asked as Luke ushered them onto the elevator.

Luke waggled his eyebrows. "He's got a thing for her," he said and nodded in the affirmative to emphasize the truthfulness of the revelation.

Marie was virtually struck speechless. "Get out" was all she could come up with.

"God's truth," Luke assured her.

"Holy cow," she breathed.

"Yep."

There was nothing else to say.

Luke drove them to the mall and cringed as they went by the scene of the crime. He parked far, far away from the site. Once at the book store, Marie helped him pick out books for Carolyn's collection.

"It's never too young to start exposing a child to good art," she informed Luke. "I read that somewhere. Look for the ones that are well illustrated."

They bought Eric Carle and Brian Wildsmith. Ezra Jack Keats and Helen Brown.

"She's got enough books now to keep her as well as a small orphanage literate and occupied for the next ten years."

"Yeah, well, you aren't the one stuck reading them to her. I want some variety before I feel compelled to do something drastic like shoot myself. How Maureen could read the same two books over and over and over again is beyond me."

Marie probed delicately. "It doesn't sound as though you, uh, had a lot in common with Carolyn's mother."

"You sure as hel—heck got that right."

"So, how come you— Never mind. None of my business." She flamed red. It was obvious Luke and Maureen hadn't had much going on an intellectual or emotional level. That only left one other plane on which a man and a woman could communicate. Carolyn's mother had evidently been "hot." Marie would have liked to have condemned him as shallow but she was living in a glass house on that one and knew it.

"Darn stupid way to communicate," Marie muttered. "We'd all have been better off taking up cold showers as an avocation."

Luke jiggled the change in his pocket. "They don't work anyway," he assured her. "The effect is remarkably short-lived." He knew. He'd taken a bunch since meeting Marie.

At least *she* hadn't been left with a child to raise as a reminder of her folly, Marie consoled herself. Luke would be paying for thinking with his hormones for a long time while Marie herself could try and get on with her l—

"Nuts," Marie said to herself. She couldn't even assure herself of getting on with her life any longer. Not until she worked up the courage to buy and use a pregnancy test kit. For all she knew, she could very well be in the same boat as Luke. Marie didn't like the idea of having anything at all in common with a member of Wade's family.

Marie reached out and covered Carolyn's ears. "Damn it," she said.

Luke looked at her curiously. "What?"

"Nothing. Just…thinking."

"Uh-oh. Carolyn's starting to fuss."

Marie looked at her watch. "She's probably getting hungry. You ready for lunch?"

Luke briefly studied the squirming mass in his arms. "You really think that's what's wrong?"

"We'll find out." Marie led the way to the food court.

They purchased chicken nuggets, fries and lemonade. "Nothing carbonated," Marie directed. "She's too young." Marie tore the nuggets and fries into small pieces and heaped them into a neat pile in front of Carolyn. Carolyn immediately grabbed a fistful. When Marie held the straw to the toddler's lips it didn't take long at all before she got the hang of it and slurped up the liquid.

"I'd say she was hungry," Marie said.

"I guess," Luke said, warily eyeing his progeny. "What a little savage."

"We'll have to work on the table manners when she gets a little bit older." Marie tried to catch her words, but they were free before she could call them back. A quick glance at Luke told her he hadn't missed the slip. He looked both relieved and…angry?

"Uh, what I meant to say…"

"Forget it. You said it and I'm holding you to it. You're going to help teach Carolyn some manners." Luke had been self-sufficient most of his life. Wade had been needy and Luke had prided himself on being the opposite, always doing for himself. But he was in over his head on this one and he didn't like it. In fact, it made him damn mad. He didn't, however, have to dwell on his inadequacies. "Before we leave the mall today you need to run into the drugstore and buy one of those do-it-yourself pregnancy test kits."

Luke shook his head. He couldn't believe he'd just said that. Talk about out of the frying pan and into the fire. He did not want to know if Marie was pregnant. He ought to pluck Carolyn out of that high chair, tuck her under his arm and run like crazy. Get as far away from Marie as quickly as he could manage. Hire a baby-sitter. It was a big world out there. Surely somebody else would know how to handle a precocious two-year-old.

But he'd promised to take Jason driving.

Was he out of his mind? Had he no instincts for self-preservation whatsoever?

Marie sighed, bringing him back to the present. "I know, I know, you're right. I'll take care of it. Avoiding the issue isn't going to make it go away."

Well, damn. She had to pick now to get cooperative and listen?

Luke knew himself. If Marie was in fact pregnant, he was in trouble. He was not a man who walked away from his troubles or responsibilities. That had been Wade. And although there wasn't a brotherly thought in his head when it came to Marie, she was family. If she needed him, Luke would come through, that's all there was to it. He had to live with himself, after all. He wouldn't like it—Luke looked at Carolyn greedily stuffing shredded chicken nuggets into her rosebud mouth and rolled his eyes—but he'd see his obligations handled properly.

And what was another eighteen years out of your life when you already had a life sentence?

"Oh, God."

"What?"

Luke shook his head. "Nothing."

Marie leaned down and picked bits of chicken off the floor, then deposited them into a napkin which she folded up into a tidy bundle for disposal. "It didn't sound like nothing," she said and offered Carolyn the straw once more.

"Well, it was. Nothing important at any rate." Just the rest of his life, or at least the only part he cared about. He'd be in his midforties by the time Carolyn and Marie's possible progeny left the house. Everybody knew there was no life after forty. He'd probably be gray and have a potbelly. What blond bombshell would want him then?

Oh, come on. Who cared about blond bombshells when he could have Marie? He was disgusted with himself. Marie had him in a constant state of semiarousal. Putting up with her for the rest of his life would not exactly be a chore. He wanted her and she was being served up to him on a silver platter. What more could a man ask? It was just hard to admit he didn't operate on a higher plane than Wade after all.

Marie shifted restlessly under Luke's stare. Had she dribbled ketchup from her fries on her shirt? What? "Are you finished?" she finally asked in desperation.

"Excuse me?" Luke snapped to. "Oh, yeah." He gestured to the place in front of Marie. "But you've barely touched your hamburger and fries."

Marie grimaced. "That was a mistake. I shouldn't have ordered anything greasy. It's making me sick."

Luke could hear his death knell tolling. Nausea again. If Marie wasn't pregnant, he'd go out and cheerfully adopt twenty more children. He only wished it was his. No, he didn't. God, he was confused.

Luke stood and cleared the table while Marie cleaned up Carolyn. Great. Fine. Might as well get it over with. "I feel

funny taking Carolyn into the men's room. She doesn't
need to see that. As long as you're here, would you take
her into the ladies' room? She's very pleased with herself
that she's stayed dry the past few days. Then we'll stop in
the drugstore on our way out,'' he announced grimly.

Marie wasn't too sure what had happened to Luke's good
mood, but it had definitely gone south. ''I'm happy to take
Carolyn to the bathroom. But if you need to get back I
can—''

Luke had Carolyn by the hand and grimly steered Marie
with the other. ''No. We're out. We're here. Let's take care
of it.''

After Marie escorted Carolyn to the bathroom, they
found the drugstore and Luke marched her down the aisle
to the appropriate feminine section. His eyes searched the
shelves and he found the right box before Marie. So intent
on the task and its possible outcome he couldn't be bothered turning red, he picked up the kit and handed it to her.
''Need anything else?''

Marie blushed and prayed for a female cashier. ''No.''

''Then let's go.''

Luke drove Marie home. When the car stopped in the
driveway, Marie picked up the drugstore bag off the seat
and opened her door. ''Thanks for coming with me. I still
don't know what to think about my gr—''

''Save it,'' Luke growled. ''I'm coming in with you.''

No way was he standing outside the bathroom door while
she—no. Marie was firm. ''This isn't necessary.'' Her
speech picked up speed. Luke was moving. ''Really.''

His door was open. ''No, I—''

He was lifting a sleeping Carolyn out of her car seat.
''Luke, stop—''

Luke came around the side of the car, Carolyn and pink
blankie in his arms. ''She can nap on the living room sofa
or one of the beds upstairs.''

"But—" She was talking to his receding back. Well, darn the man. Marie chased after him.

Luke was a man on a mission. He turned when he reached the front door. "Got your key? Hurry up. She's a dead weight when she's asleep."

Marie gave up. Luke was doing a great imitation of a steamroller. She could either jump on board and ride or she could get smushed underneath the roller. She opened the door.

Luke strode purposefully into the living room. "Here. Put the back cushions onto the floor in front of the sofa. That'll give her more room and if she rolls, she'll land on something soft."

Marie did as she was told, wondering all the while what kind of landing she herself would have if she allowed Luke to continue horning in on her life.

Carolyn was quickly settled on the sofa. Luke covered her with the waffle-weave blanket she'd so quickly formed an attachment to. She stirred sleepily, found her thumb and went right back under.

Luke settled himself into the oversize faded green-and-gold floral wingback chair her grandfather used to claim and looked at Marie expectantly. "Well?"

"Well, what?" Marie snapped back.

He gestured to the bag still in her hand. "Go use it."

She threw it onto the slate coffee table as though it might bite. "Later. I want to talk about my gra—"

But Luke wanted to know what fate held in store for him and he wanted to know right then. He shook his head. "Now."

What a bully. What a jerk. Marie crossed her arms stubbornly and stared.

Luke rose, picked up the bag and pressed it into her hand. "Come on. The suspense is killing me. I'll take Jason driving this afternoon when he gets home from school. Promise."

This was embarrassing. It was mortifying. She barely knew this man. Marie heaved a hefty sigh. But if he took Jason driving it would be a fair exchange. She took herself upstairs.

Luke was seriously thinking about going after her ten minutes later. How long did the stupid test take for crying out loud? Was she sick again? Had she fainted? Damn it all, how inconsiderate could she be to leave him hanging like this? Marie damn well better be passed out on the floor or sick as a dog up there. Luke began drumming with his fingers on the armchair, debating as to whether he should go barging upstairs or not.

He was just pushing himself out of the chair when Marie walked back in another five minutes later.

"Luke?" She spoke softly out of deference for the sleeping child although she felt more like screaming.

Luke rose and faced her. This must be how a man felt facing a firing squad. "What?"

Marie gave him a helpless look.

"What?" he repeated more urgently, although he already suspected her answer.

Her lips worked but no sound came out.

Luke had a bit of a fatalistic streak in him and he knew. Hell, he'd known when she'd first mentioned the possibility the day before. "It was positive, wasn't it?"

She nodded. "It turned blue," she finally said.

"You're having a boy?" Luke asked.

"No. If the stick turns blue it means you're pregnant. Boy or girl. Either one."

Luke sank heavily back into the old wingback. Oh, yes, he'd known but somehow he was still stunned.

Marie was pregnant.

He was going to be a father.

Again.

Well, damn.

Chapter Seven

"There's only one thing to do," Luke informed Marie grimly.

Marie held up a defensive hand. "I'm not getting rid of it," she warned him. "I don't know how I'm going to handle everything just yet." That was the understatement of the year. "But everything will come out okay in the wash, just see if it doesn't." Dear God, please let it come out in the wash, she pleaded.

Marie needed calming down. So did Luke, but first things first. "Of course everything's going to be okay. And I wasn't going to suggest aborting the little tike. You should know me better than that."

"I barely know you at all."

She would, she certainly would before too much longer. Luke made a placating gesture. "Now, you need to calm down. Getting all upset can't be good for the baby. He'll be born with a permanent startle reflex. No point in having a nervous breakdown over what you can't change." Good advice. He ought to listen to it himself.

"God never sends more than you can bear," Marie informed him as though she were reciting catechism.

"And He never shuts a door without opening a window," Luke repeated dutifully.

Marie pointed a finger at him. "Exactly." She started pacing the length of the room. "We may not understand the why of it, but that's not important. What counts is that you play out the cards life deals. You can't give up and fold."

Luke rolled his eyes as Marie continued to roll out one cliché after another. Good grief.

"I'll tell you one thing," Marie announced as she pivoted and began her umpteenth trip across the living room.

"What's that?" Luke asked, humoring her.

"I've handled things so far and believe you me, there are an inordinate amount of jokers in the deck the fates have been dealing from lately."

Tell me about it, Luke thought, but wisely kept his mouth shut.

"But I've handled things just fine. Just fine. And I'll continue to handle any other...whatever life sees fit to throw my way, see if I don't."

It was the whatever part that had him worried. Luke was still reeling from the last few blows fate had dealt him recently. He hated to think what else might be in store. In fact, Luke refused to ponder it at all. Here and now was enough. Sufficient unto the day are the troubles...whatever. Anyway, he'd take care of today and worry about tomorrow when tomorrow came.

"Fine. We'll play out what we've been dealt. We'll get married. That ought to trump fate's high cards. I'll check into things and see how quickly we can accomplish it." Luke told himself it was a magnanimous offer and he assumed Marie would appreciate his generosity.

"You've got to go with the flow in life," Marie continued. "If you don't bend, you'll br— What?"

"I said we'll get married." And every night he would do his best be a husband to her in every way. Lord, he was depraved. All right, so it wouldn't be such a sacrifice to sleep with Marie. Did that make it any less noble? Did it? Marie would still be taken care of, wouldn't she? Of course she would. He scowled, irritated with himself. A candy-coated pill was still a pill, after all. He was altruistic, darn it, a real prince of a guy. Great sex would simply be...a side benefit, that was all.

Though normally gregarious, Marie was, for the first time in her recollection, struck dumb. Bug-eyed, she stared at Luke, her mouth working like a fish. "What?" she finally gasped a second time, positive she'd heard wrong. He couldn't have just proposed marriage. Not with that scowl on his face.

"You heard me," Luke said irritably. "I'm not repeating it a third time."

"Generally speaking, when a man asks a woman to be his wife—"

"I'm not asking," Luke pointed out. "We were playing cards, remember?"

Marie ignored him. "When a man asks a woman to be his wife, he at least makes some kind of attempt to be pleasant about it." She'd still say no, but honestly, the man could at least ask nicely. Every woman had romantic illusions and dearly held fantasies regarding her marriage proposals. Life with Wade had been hell, but damn it all, at least his proposal had been good. There'd been flowers and illegal champagne for the underage lovers. Wade had hidden the ring in a piece of chocolate. Now that was romance.

Luke, on the other hand, knew absolutely nothing about a woman's fantasy life, Marie decided. In fact, Luke had the finesse of an elephant picking his way through a field of daisies.

Luke grabbed an arm as she whizzed by, stopping Marie

in her tracks. "Don't be stupid," he lectured, irritated with her lack of gratitude.

"Oh, that's good. Calling me stupid is bound to make me want to marry you." Marie glanced heavenward as if to see if anyone was taking note of this mortal's stupidity.

Luke lightly shook her. "You're going to have to be sensible about this, Marie. It's the only workable solution."

"Sensible! *I'm* not being sensible? There is very little basis for marriage here, Luke. For heaven's sake, I don't even like you all that much."

"That's all right. I don't much care for you, either. We're talking marriage here, not bosom buddies." Darn, he would have to bring up bosoms. Now he was thinking about hers again.

She was dealing with a lunatic. It was the only possible explanation. One had to speak to the mentally deranged calmly. It wouldn't do to get them all stirred up and have them totally flip out on you. "Are you nuts? Are you crazy? We've just admitted we don't particularly care for each other and in your mind that's grounds for marriage?"

Luke was disgusted. There was no reasoning with a female. The woman was totally irrational. "Given the circumstances, yes."

Marie threw up her hands. "I don't believe this. Luke, for your information marriage requires a certain amount of liking. Call them crazy but in this day and age most participants actually insist on being in love before taking the big step."

"Like you loved Wade."

Marie swung around and pointed. "Yes. Like that. I would not have married your brother if I hadn't thought I loved him."

"And that lasted for—how long?"

"All right, so I had a slightly skewed perspective on what love was back then and sometimes things don't exactly work out, still—"

Luke grabbed her again. Honestly, the woman was going to wear a strip out of the carpet. "Marie, there's an old song about getting married when you're all fevered up and wild. But eventually the fire goes out and you're left with nothing but ashes. All we're doing is skipping the first step. And it's not like it's not for a good cause."

"Let me get this straight. We're to skip all the silly preliminary stuff like being in love, caring for each other, that kind of thing and just go right to the part where the bloom is off the rose and we're indifferent about each other? This is supposed to be an improvement over most other couples?"

Luke began pacing himself. "Your problem is, your hormones are all in a dither. You're not thinking clearly."

Marie put a hand over her heart and pretended to swoon. "Oh, be still my beating heart. Watch it, Luke, I'm not sure I can handle all this romance and the endearing blandishments you've got me knee deep in."

She'd struck a nerve. Luke had never been like Wade, able to turn on the charm at the drop of a hat. It had always bothered him that women couldn't seem to see through all that sloppy, unnecessary stuff to what was important. Okay, so his tongue didn't drip honey. He also had one heck of a lot more stability than some lousy fragile honeycomb. *He'd* come home every night. In time for dinner. *His* breath wouldn't smell of booze and his body wouldn't have picked up the scent of some other woman's perfume. *His* paycheck would make it home with him. Intact. *He'd* remember to put out the trash on Tuesday mornings. *Whoa!* Put the garbage out? Oh for— Luke scowled and struggled to reign in his escalating temper. "How old are you?"

"Twenty-three, your point being—?."

"You should be beyond all that at your age," he loftily informed her.

Beyond needing love? Who got past that? At any age?

"It's only the past hundred years or so that love has even

been an issue in marriage. If you knew your history you'd know that. Marriages were for political connections, land, that kind of thing.''

"I am not a Kennedy, so you can forget any political connections and I own absolutely nothing. Not even so much as a mortgage. I'm afraid you're totally out of luck.''

"Maybe not. With us it would be a little more intangible in what we'd each gain, but think about it.'' Luke began ticking items off on his fingers. "You could stay at home if you wanted, take care of the baby. And if you did that, it wouldn't be that big of a deal for you to watch Carolyn while you were at it. You're a lot better with her than I am.''

Marie's eyes widened and her hand went to her chest in classic *Who me?* sort of gesture. He was marrying her to gain a built-in baby-sitter? What a clod.

Luke saw the burgeoning protest. "Wait,'' he cautioned. "Let me finish.'' He waited until her mouth closed and her eyes came back down to size. Scrambling frantically he tried to come up with more, logical, rational reasons for why they should marry. Luke had always believed such decisions should be based on reason. Reason gave the institution of marriage a foundation. Didn't Marie understand that? You had to have a foundation on which to build a relationship. The fact that he wanted her to the point of developing a constant ache wasn't enough. In fact, it scared him silly.

"Like I said, you could help me out with Carolyn, at least for as long as you're home. If you decide you'd like to work, we can figure out something else. That's one.'' Luke moved on to a second finger. "My house has a first-floor guest bedroom. Your grandfather could stay there and not have to do any stairs while he's recovering.'' Inspired, he added, "You know, he's getting older. He should probably be thinking about limiting his stairs altogether.'' Luke gestured around. "We could rent this place out for a while if we wanted. Get your grandfather a little extra income."

Marie wondered if Luke realized he'd called his home simply a house. Was it just a slip or was there something deeper there?

Like what?

How about an innate loneliness? A disconnection or feeling of alienation from the rest of the world.

Oh, how ridiculous. Look at her getting all Freudian. Still, though, Marie couldn't help but feel a bit more sympathetic. After all, it could be the man didn't say the right things because he simply didn't know how to communicate. It was sad when she thought about it and certainly his heart was in the right place, wasn't it?

Oblivious to Marie's mental musings, Luke continued ticking off fingers. "And there's Jason. Can't forget him."

She wished.

"Don't get your water all in a boil, but the truth is I think I'm a little better at handling him."

That wasn't saying much.

"I'm not criticizing, after all you're better with Carolyn. I'm just saying I could give you a hand there. At the least see him through to his license."

It was darn tempting. "Uh-huh. Luke, this is all well and good but—"

"I'm still not done."

"Oh, for heaven's sake."

"Give me a minute here. I've still got the most important one of all left."

Marie cocked a hand on her hip. "Well?"

Luke spread his hands wide. "The baby, Marie. The baby. I've got a responsibility to my own flesh and blood, don't I?" Of course he did. That was his niece or nephew cooking in there. "Speaking of which, shouldn't you be sitting down or something? Putting your feet up? I think pregnant ladies have to watch out for swollen ankles. At least I remember Maureen complaining about them.''

"Let me worry about my ankles, all right? And believe me, this child is not your responsibility. He or she is not your flesh and blood. I'd have noticed if you'd been there for the conception, trust me on this.'' Man, would she have noticed.

"Marie—''

"No. Now it's your turn to listen. You think I don't see what's happening here? You've got some kind of Sir Galahad complex going. You've got me cast as a modern-day maiden in distress and you're right. I am. But modern-day princesses save themselves, they don't sit around and wait for Prince Charming.''

Carolyn was snuggled under her blankie while she gently sucked on her thumb. Marie had to smile and touched her stomach. God, she hoped her own progeny was half as cute. She gestured to the sleeping child. "Don't worry about me, Luke. You're already taking care of your responsibilities. I doubt Wade would have, even if he'd lived, but that's my problem. I'll handle this thing by myself.''

"This wouldn't be the first time I'd be there to pick up the pieces of someone else's mistake. I'm getting used to it. Look, Marie—'' Luke gave a frustrated glance in Carolyn's direction then took Marie's elbow and steered her toward the back of the house and away from the sleeping child. "Let's get you a glass of milk. Seems to me you're supposed to be drinking a lot of milk now.'' Once in the kitchen he opened the refrigerator and began rummaging through.

Marie opened the dishwasher and took out a clean cup. "Okay, okay. You win. Give me the dumb milk and I'll sit down with my feet up but I'm still not marrying you.''

Luke poured the liquid and settled her in a chair. He waited for her to pick up the glass. "It's not taking advantage if I let you.''

She sipped. "Still—"

"There's no still about it," Luke said pouring himself some milk for lack of anything better to do with his hands. God, it had been years since he'd drunk milk. Bravely he chugged it down and remembered why he'd stopped drinking it. He hated milk. It was all he could do not to gag. "There's something I have to tell you."

"You're gay and marriage to me would just be a front. No, thank you."

He glared at her and she laughed. "Just kidding."

"Not funny."

"No, I guess not." And he was right. It wouldn't be funny, it would be criminal. Luke was entirely too prime a specimen and it would be a shame if some woman couldn't have him. "So, what's the big secret?"

"Don't worry about taking advantage. I've been had by a far far better source than you."

"Meaning?" Marie put her feet up on the chair next to hers at the kitchen table. Her ankles weren't swollen but it still felt good. She picked up her glass again.

"Carolyn's not mine."

"Yeah, right."

"I'm serious here. Carolyn is in no way related to me."

Marie sprayed liquid all over and began choking. "What? What?"

Luke rushed over and began pounding her on the back. "You all right?"

She about coughed up her lungs. "You're not supposed to hit somebody on the back when they're choking," she sputtered. "Not unless they can't speak, cough or breathe. Then you get behind them and do abdominal thrusts. You still don't whack them on the back." She took a napkin from the dispenser and dabbed at the milk dripping off her chin and blouse front.

"See? See? I didn't know that. What if Carolyn chokes and I hit her on the back? What if something else happens and I do the wrong thing? I am not being a martyr here, Marie. I need you." There. He'd finally admitted it out loud. He just hadn't admitted to all the ways he needed—wanted her.

Marie's heart gave a lurch in her chest at those words. Luke was one hunk of man. To be truly *needed* by him, well... But no, that kind of thinking would lead only to disaster. "Tell me about Carolyn," she said instead. "She's really not yours?"

"In every way that matters she's mine," Luke said. "And she's staying mine. Nothing's going to change that." His back was to her as he opened an upper cabinet and checked the contents.

Marie wished he'd turn around. She wanted to see his face. "Don't leave me hanging here, Luke. You can't drop a bomb like that and then clam up."

Luke grunted when he opened the second cabinet door. Cookies. Not his favorites—he'd prefer a handful of Oreos, but these would do. He brought the cellophane-wrapped package over to the table and straddled the chair next to hers. Taking a cookie, he examined it carefully then demolished it in one bite.

"Luke," Marie all but wailed. "Come on!"

"All right, already. You saw my house. It's obvious I haven't lived here all that long. You didn't even know I'd moved."

"Last I heard you were in Fort Wayne."

"And before that, Kalamazoo."

Marie snatched the cookie he was gesturing with and stuffed it in her mouth. "I just know this is leading somewhere," she mumbled around the crumbs.

"Patience," Luke advised. "And you really should watch the empty calories now, you know? There must be an apple or an orange around here somewhere." He twisted on the chair and began to scan the countertops.

"I am going to murder you in about ten seconds flat."

Luke was forced to reluctantly smile. Didn't she realize the ridiculousness of someone her size threatening someone with his height and breadth? "Yes, this is leading somewhere," he soothed as he rose and fetched an apple from a bowl he'd spotted. "While I was in Kalamazoo, I worked with a young lady named Maureen." He proffered the apple.

She took it. "Carolyn's mother."

"Right. She was the receptionist, maybe a year or two out of high school. We'd say hello to each other as I went in or out, that kind of thing."

"Passing acquaintances."

"Exactly. Gradually we reached the point where we'd stop and talk a bit before we'd go about our business. Nice kid."

"You never touched her." Marie wanted to be clear on that point.

"Never."

"But somebody else did."

"She had a boyfriend and she was in L-O-V-E."

"You don't have to spell it. *Love.* It's a perfectly acceptable word for all that it does have four letters." Marie took a vicious bite out of the apple.

"You're entitled to your opinion. But to get back to the story—"

Marie swallowed. "Please do."

Luke ignored her. "For about six months Maureen absolutely sparkled every time you saw her. Before you knew it, she had a ring with a stone the size a robin would have been proud to lay."

"Was it real?"

"Diamond? Probably not. Everybody assumed it was cubic zirconia. Nobody bothered to voice our suspicions to Maureen." Luke shrugged. "It didn't matter."

"Not to you." But Maureen might have cared if anyone had bothered to inform her.

Luke rolled his eyes. "Could I finish here? Thank you. She thought she was engaged, that's all that matters now."

Marie continued to munch her way methodically around the apple. "Okay, so she's engaged. Then what?"

"One day she came to work with the side of her face all bruised up, limping."

Marie's eyebrows rose. "From what as if I don't know already."

"She said she'd slipped on a patch of ice and taken a bad fall. It was winter. We all bought it. Told her to be more careful. She hobbled around for a week or two and seemed to be okay again, although in retrospect a lot of the sparkle was gone."

"Yeah?"

"Then she called in sick. Missed three days. When she came back she still had the remnants of a black eye. Thought she'd covered it up with makeup. There's no way you could cover a shiner that size." Luke shook his head at Maureen's naïveté. "I realized she'd taken to wearing long-sleeved blouses that buttoned all the way up and those knit things with the tubey necks that kind of roll over back on themselves, you know?"

"Turtlenecks?"

"That's it. Turtlenecks. Told myself she could just be hiding hickeys, but I didn't really believe it. I never had any sisters but it wasn't all that hard to imagine how I'd feel if something like that was happening to one and no-body tried to help. So, anyway, this one day when I couldn't stand it any longer I took her out to lunch and had a long talk with her. Explained how anyone who would hit a woman was lower than a snake's belly, how it would probably only get worse if she actually married the jerk and how she deserved better. Set her up with the company counselor."

"You did all that?"

Luke shifted restlessly. "What was I supposed to do?

Let the guy continue to use her for drum practice? She was bigger than you, sturdy looking, but still—''

Marie reached over and grasped his hand. "You did the right thing. It's just that most people don't want to get involved. Especially not in something ugly like that.''

Luke stared at her, oddly uncomfortable with her praise. "Uh—anyway, the long and short of it, is she gave him back the cubic zirconia. He stalked her a bit but a police order was enough to get him to back off, thank God.''

"She never saw him again?''

"Not after the first arrest.''

"The first—never mind. I don't want to know. You handled it and it worked. Good.''

"Well, it's not quite good yet. What happened next was, she discovered she was pregnant.''

"Good grief. Carolyn?''

Luke nodded. "Yeah, only it wasn't Carolyn yet. She was barely beginning to bake at that point. Maureen came to me all hysterical again—why do women do that? They have to know men can't take tears and they do it anyway.''

Marie patted his arm. "We're a diabolical group, I admit it. Not to worry, though. I promise I'll never cry in front of you. Keep going.''

"I took her back up to the counselor. Maureen finally admitted she was afraid the ex wouldn't stay banished if he knew about the baby. She was already into the protective mamma syndrome. It was one thing for *el boyfriendo* to knock Maureen around. No way was he touching her child. So she comes to me again—calmer this time. I figure she knew I was going to bolt if she started crying again. Tells me she doesn't want to use his name on the birth certificate. Would it be all right if she used mine instead?''

"Wow." Marie sat back in her chair. "Why didn't she just leave it blank?''

"She figured he could still put two and two together. If my name was listed as the father, there was no way he could claim the baby. He'd just think she'd gone right from one man to another and was easy. Maybe knock her around a bit more, but he'd leave the kid alone.''

Marie was incredulous. "And you said yes?''

"It didn't seem like that big a deal. All she wanted was protection for her baby. No support or anything like that, although if she'd asked I'd probably have tried to help her out. I transferred to Fort Wayne a little while later. Never even saw the baby. I left before she'd come back from maternity leave. Didn't hear from her for three years. I'd practically forgotten the whole thing, then wham, out of nowhere comes a notification from Department of Children and Family Services to come pick up my daughter. Maureen had died. Evidently she had no other relatives. It was my name on the birth certificate, so here I am—instant daddy.''

"Holy smoke. It's a darn good thing, too. The other alternatives don't bear thinking about. She'd have either been turned over to an abusive father or dumped into the system, poor little tike.''

"How about spreading a little of that sympathy this way?''

Marie rose and deposited the apple core in the trash, her cup in the sink. "Oh, you're a big strong man. You don't need sympathy. You can handle Carolyn with one hand tied behind your back. Why, you probably eat nails for breakfast.'' Marie meant it. There was iron in Luke's backbone. He had a physical strength to his body that left her annoyingly breathless and she was beginning to see a strength in his character she couldn't help but admire.

A thump sounded from the front of the house.

Marie jumped. "What was that?''

Luke was already moving. "Carolyn!'' was all he said.

They both raced down the hall, Luke well in the lead. He used a hand on the old-fashioned doorway trim as a pivot point and swung into the living room. A very sleepy, disoriented toddler blinked up at him. She lay on the cushions they'd removed from the sofa and set on the floor in front of the sofa for just such an eventuality.

Luke made a conscious effort to slow down then. He didn't want to startle her. She wasn't crying and he did not want to trigger any tears by scaring her and acting like a lunatic. He swallowed hard in an effort to dislodge his heart, which was currently stuck in his throat, and force it back down into his chest where it belonged. He took a calming breath, then Marie came charging full tilt around the corner and crashed into his back.

"What? What happened?"

Luke steadied her, but other than that, he ignored her. His focus was on his child. He made an attempt at smiling as he approached the sofa. "What'd you do, baby girl? Roll off the couch?" He knelt beside Carolyn and lightly massaged her limbs. Partially it was an attempt to soothe the toddler but mostly it served to assure himself she was all right.

His blood was gradually slowing its frantic rush through his temples. As best he could determine, Carolyn was just fine. "Might as well stay down where you are," he murmured. "You can sleep on the pillows as well as the sofa." Luke retucked the blanket up around her neck so she could feel the satiny ribbon binding against her cheek. He had already discovered its presence soothed the two-year-old and rightly assumed it would help in this strange environment. Then he began rubbing her back.

Carolyn's eyes were already rolling in her head as she struggled to stay awake long enough to have her insatiable curiosity satisfied. "Daddy?"

"I'm right here."

"Whose house dis?"

"This is Marie's house," he informed her in what he hoped was a hypnotic murmur. "And you, little girl, can barely keep your eyes open. Why don't you close them and finish your nap? When you wake up maybe Marie will help us bake cookies, hmm? What do you think?''

He grinned as Carolyn stared at him with eyes rapidly glazing over.

''If she's too busy we'll toodle on back to our own house and give it a try ourselves. They probably won't be edible, but you wouldn't care, would you, sweetie? I read in one of the kid manuals I picked up that process counts for more than product and hands-on experiences were very important for your development. You agree with that?''

Carolyn blinked up at him once, twice, then her black lashes settled permanently on her delicately flushed cheeks.

Luke lightened the massaging motion on her back. After about a minute more he carefully lifted his hand all together. Carolyn didn't budge. He leaned down to kiss her cheek, changed his mind when he realized the kiss was more for him than the sleeping child and might, in fact, awaken her again. He edged away. Luke turned to find Marie smiling at him.

He flushed. ''What?''

Marie shrugged. ''Nothing. You're very sweet with her.''

He was insulted. No man wanted the woman he lusted after to think of him as sweet, for crying out loud. Hot. Studly. Those were manly adjectives, not sweet. ''Don't be any more stupid than you can help. Sweet,'' he practically snorted. ''There's not a sweet bone in my body.''

''If you say so,'' Marie agreed equitably. ''However, I would like to point out the consideration and care you're taking to creep out of the room quietly so you don't wake her up again.''

The woman was as dense as the fog that sometimes rolled in all the way from Lake Michigan. ''That's not being considerate. That's self-preservation. She wakes up before she's good and ready and she'll be cranky all afternoon. I've already learned that the hard way. As you will recall from the day we picked her up, the woman has a temper.''

"That she does."

"It only makes sense to take steps to avoid one of her screaming meemies imitations."

"Absolutely."

"Shut up."

Behind his back, Marie grinned the entire trip down the hall.

"Want some coffee?" she asked once back in the kitchen.

"Yeah, I guess." Luke settled heavily back into a kitchen chair. "When will Jason be home?"

Marie glanced at the wall clock while she fiddled with the coffeemaker. "Another half an hour."

Luke nodded. "I'll take him driving when he gets in if you're up to watching Carolyn while we're gone."

"No problem. I don't mind baking cookies. Jason will appreciate them." She reached up into a cabinet and brought down two mugs. Marie retrieved the milk from the refrigerator, the sugar bowl from its hiding place. The smell of brewing coffee began to permeate the air.

Luke was just about to remark on the wonderful aroma when Marie suddenly began supporting herself with one hand on the countertop and put the other hand over her mouth. "Ugh," she said.

Luke hurriedly rose. Once again his adrenaline coursed. Fight or flight, which one? Who knew? God, his body was going to be little better than a train wreck in nothing flat at this rate. "Are you going to faint, Marie? You wouldn't do that to me, would you? Talk to me. What's the matter?"

She took her hand off her mouth just long enough to gesture toward the coffeemaker. "This was a mistake."

Luke glanced over, saw nothing out of the ordinary. "What? What was a mistake?"

"Can't you smell it? The coffee. Something's wrong

with it. The odor is making me sick." Marie gagged. "Scratch that. It's killing me."

Luke took a deep sniff. "There's nothing wrong with the coffee, Marie."

"There has to be."

"No," he said regretfully. "The change is with you. It's affecting you differently now that you're pregnant. Remember how the hamburger smell got to you last night?" He took the pot from its stand, looked at it longingly then bravely poured it down the drain. He'd really wanted that coffee. He'd planned to use it to wash the disgusting milk taste out of his mouth. Instead, he ran the water to rinse the coffee all the way down and opened the window over the sink.

"My grandfather's air-conditioning was designed for the square footage of the house. The entire out-of-doors is a bit beyond its capacity."

"Ah, the ultimate proof of pregnancy. You're already sounding like a mother. Must be all those maternal hormones at work. Unfortunately, airing the place out is the quickest way to get rid of the smell that's bothering you."

Marie's supporting hand had collapsed. Now she was using both elbows on the countertop. She wanted to tell him to shut up but she didn't have the energy. "Luke, what's really happening here? You don't need me to watch Carolyn for you. True, you'll need a quality day care once you go back to work, but otherwise you've already gotten quite good with her."

"There's a long way to go," he insisted as he shut off the tap.

"Yes, but you'd make it."

"Maybe. Probably." He'd allow for the slim possibility and it wasn't good for Marie to know how terrified he was of making a mistake in Carolyn's upbringing—he didn't want her to grow up emotionally or physically damaged somehow. And he may not have had any sisters but he'd picked up a few pointers on handling women through the years. For one thing, you did not infer, ever, that you thought they were anything less than Superwoman. You did your protecting and caretaking on the sly or you faced charges of caveman tactics. "Just like you'll probably pull yourself through your grandfather's crisis, Jason's license and the baby and be just fine without me..." Yeah, right. "But is it so wrong for us to lean on each other? That way neither one of us runs the risk of falling on our face. I mean, isn't this what the development of societies and civilizations is all about?" It sounded good to him. "The human race as a whole has developed well past the point where any individual has to do it all. Division of labor. Cooperation. That's what it's all about. You weave baskets, I'll trade some of my corn to get one. Then I'll go down the road and barter some of my hides for a water pot." Luke slapped his leg, really getting into it. "It's a damn good idea, Marie. Think about it. Why fly in the face of thousands of years of evolution?"

Good grief. Now he was turning his marriage proposal into a lesson in sociology. Marie stared at him thoughtfully for a good long while. He was irresistible when he was earnest.

"Okay," she finally said.

"Okay?"

She nodded slowly. "I want you to know I have grave reservations about this, but yes. Okay."

"Well, then," he said, elated. "That's okay. You won't be sorry." And neither would he.

Chapter Eight

Marie regretted her acceptance of Luke's proposal as soon as the coffee fumes dissipated. What had she been thinking of? She already had two difficult-to-handle men in her life. Why in the world would she take on a third? Especially the brother of her former husband. She hadn't learned her lesson the first time about the Deforest men? She had to go back and hit her head against the same brick wall a second time? The way her life was headed she'd be able to shortly hire on as a writer for a soap opera. There'd be no worries over creativity or inspiration, that was for sure. She was accumulating enough to draw on from her real-life reserves to last for a lifetime of a daytime serial. The only problem Marie could foresee was plausibility. Her real life would stretch even a soap opera audience's believability index.

But how to tell the prospective groom that his fiancé of ten minutes had already changed her mind?

Marie believed she'd grown and matured since her last attempt at marriage. She'd become strong. So how come she couldn't get her mouth to open to inform Luke of her change of heart?

"Ah, Luke—"

"Hey, I'm home," came Jason's voice from the doorway. "Whose car is out in fr... Hey, Luke, it's you. How's it going, man?" With a dull thump speaking of heaviness, Jason dropped his backpack on the floor by the kitchen door. "Think you could take me driving now, Luke? I've got my permit on me."

"Jason," Marie said reprovingly. "Pick your book bag up off the floor. The school year has barely begun and you're already dropping things as you come in the door."

"Yeah, yeah. Whatever."

"Carolyn's sleeping in the front room, so please lower your voice. And don't forget to get your ice pack out of your lunch box and put it back into the freezer so you can use it again tomorrow."

"See?" Luke said. "You're a natural. You're already in the groove."

"Natural what?" Jason queried. "Marie can't groove. She's too square."

Marie made a face at Jason's back. It was all she could see. Having stepped unconcernedly over the backpack in question, his front side was now getting up close and personal with the contents of the refrigerator. Grabbing a quart of milk, an apple, a bag of baby carrots and a container of yogurt, Jason backed out of the refrigerator and kicked the door shut. "Man, there's never anything to eat here." He set his booty on the countertop and took down a box of graham crackers from the cabinet. "You need to go grocery shopping, Marie."

"Jason, you need to at least make a pretense of a little small talk. You don't walk in the door and immediately ask Luke to take you driving."

"Why not?" Jason asked and drank milk directly from the carton.

"Jason!"

"What now?"

"Use a cup. And mark that milk carton so the rest of us know not to use it."

"Why? I'm not sick or anything. Cups are stupid and a waste of time. If I use one you're only going to tell me to wash it and get all mad when I don't," Jason replied in what he probably thought was all reasonableness. "I'm just trying to save us an argument. If you'd stop and think about it, you should be thanking me for drinking out of the carton, not jumping all over me. And I don't see why it's rude to talk about Luke taking me driving without making a lot of dumb small talk first. What am I supposed to do, talk about the weather? It's not like he's stupid or anything. I mean, not totally. I bet he already knows it's sunny and hot."

"Hey, how about those Bears?" Luke murmured only to earn two glares.

"The clue phone is ringing, and I think it's for you, Marie. Come on, why else would he be here if it wasn't to take me driving? For sure there's nothing else going on around this dump that's worth his time." Jason gestured with the milk carton. "Look at him. Look at yourself. He's big league, Marie. Not to hurt your feelings or anything but you're...not even triple A. The way I see it, there's no point in beating around the bush. The sooner we go driving, the sooner he gets to blow this place off. God knows I would if I could."

Luke cleared his throat. Jason was certainly blind when it came to his niece's charms. "Actually, there are one or two other points of interest here other than you, Jase. As a matter of fact, your uh, niece—why does that sound so strange?" Luke shook his head and continued. "Forget it. Anyway, Marie had just agreed to marry me when you walked in."

The quart of milk slipped through Jason's hands. He caught himself and it in the nick of time. "What?"

Stunned, Jason stared from one to the other. "You're kidding, right?"

It wasn't often you could stun an adolescent speechless. Marie, who moments before had been on the brink of reneging, savored the moment. "No, he's not kidding." And if this wasn't a totally juvenile reason for going through with a marriage, to spite your uncle, she didn't know what was.

You'd think Luke was asking him to accept some long, complicated Einsteinian formula explaining the existence of antimatter instead of the simple bald statement he'd made. Marie and Luke were to marry. How hard was that to understand?

"You and—" Jason gestured at Luke "—married?" His voice all but squeaked.

Luke began to frown. "Yeah. She and me. Married. What of it?"

Jason set the milk down on the counter and turned his back to them. "Nothing. It's fine. Couldn't be better. I hope you're happy together and you certainly don't have to worry about me. Dad and me'll be fine. We don't need you. We don't need anybody."

"Jason—"

"You'll at least wait until he's back home, won't you, Marie? Not that it matters to me 'cause it doesn't, but Dad'll probably want to see you get hitched an' all."

"Jason, I'm not moving out."

Jason swung around. "You're not?"

"No." Marie grimaced. "Well, actually, yes I am, but you and Grandpa are coming with me."

"Marie, you don't take your family with you when you get married. That's why people get married in the first place. To get away from their family."

The boy had a lot to learn, Luke decided. "Not always" was all he said. "Marie and I have no intention of leaving you or your dad behind. We figured it'd be easier on your father to have a first-floor bedroom for a while. That's why you'll all come to my house. The hallways are wider, the bathrooms larger. If he has to use a walker for a little while, he's less likely to get tangled up with it at my place."

"You think he'll have to have a walker?"

"Maybe. For a while."

"Man, that'll look great in front of my friends."

"We could always keep him locked up and out of sight until he was totally well."

Jason chewed his lip and appeared to give the idea some thought.

"I was kidding."

He sighed. "They already know he's way older than their dads anyway so I guess it doesn't matter. I don't know about moving, though."

Luke shrugged. "It's the same high school district so that wouldn't be a problem." Then he threw in the kicker. "And I had a surround sound system installed when the place was being built." Luke picked up a set of car keys from the countertop and jingled them a bit. "Now, do you want to go driving or what?"

Jason whooped and Marie shushed him. Luke made him move the book bag away from the traffic pattern although it remained on the floor. The cold pack was taken out of the lunch-bag-size soft-sided cooler and put in the freezer as well. "Anything else?" Luke asked with an arched brow. He and Jason were poised by the back door, Jason practically quivering as he waited for the release.

Marie sighed and waved them off. She'd wipe the cookie crumbs and the handful of mashed grapes off the inside walls of his lunch tote herself. She'd also deal with actually getting the backpack off the floor once they were gone. She was lucky to have gotten as much as she had and was grateful.

"No, go ahead. Just bring the car back in one piece, all right?"

"Things," Jason said as he snatched the keys out of Luke's hand. "The car is just a thing, remember, Marie? You're always telling me that things aren't important in life. It's people that count."

"If that car isn't in one piece when you get back," Marie called after his receding form, "you won't stay in one for long after I get a hold of you, Jason Fort. You just think about that."

"What'd you say, Marie? I can't heeaaarrr you." Jason was already rounding the side of the building, headed for the street.

"Try not to worry," Luke said as he followed more slowly. "He's with me. I'll put the fear of God in him if he gets reckless."

Marie felt her first frisson of alarm. Jason could be a pain, but he was still a blood relative and Marie protected her own. "Uh, Luke? Maybe we should talk before you go out."

"I told you not to worry. Have a little faith, would you?"

The door no sooner closed when Carolyn woke up. She came wandering into the kitchen, her pink blanket over her shoulders like a shawl, a thumb in her mouth.

"Hi, sweetie," Marie greeted her. "Did you have a good sleep?"

Carolyn blinked like an owl and considered the question. "Where's Daddy?"

"Daddy went out with Jason for a little while. They'll be back before you know it."

Marie thought fast as Carolyn's face began to cloud up. Poor little tike, waking up in a strange place and her already beloved daddy among the missing.

"You know what I think?" Marie asked, hoping to distract the child before the tears began. She'd already seen little schnookums in action once and once was definitely enough. Marie could happily go a long while without at-

tempting to deal with another two-year-old temper tantrum
à la the type she'd witnessed in Kalamazoo.

"What?" Carolyn asked, the first fat tear already trem-
bling on the edge of her filled lower lid.

"I bet Daddy and Jason will be hungry when they get
back." She didn't think any such thing. Luke would probably be nauseous if Jason took more than two corners while
they were out together. Food would be the last thing on his
mind. In fact, Marie seriously considered turning the ther-
mostat up. Hadn't she read somewhere that victims of
shock tended to feel cold? It might be best to be prepared.

Carolyn pointed to her chest. "I'm hungwy, too," she
said, drawing Marie back from her mental musings.

"Of course you are. Napping's tough work. How about
if you and I bake some cookies?"

Carolyn nodded enthusiastically. "I help," she said
firmly.

Marie knelt down and gave Carolyn a hug and a kiss on
the top of her head. "Thank you. What would I do without
you? I'd have to make the cookies all by myself."

Carolyn wrapped her pudgy arms around Marie's neck
and squeezed. A boa constrictor could take lessons. She
reached up and loosened Carolyn's grip. "Easy does it,
cutie. Marie's got to breathe."

Carolyn beamed. "You funny."

"Humor, like beauty, must be in the eye of the be-
holder," Marie muttered to herself as she rose. "How about
peanut butter? You think Daddy likes peanut butter cookies?" Peanuts are good for you. Lots of protein. She
thought about using jelly to make them sandwich cookies.
Fruit, you know.

Carolyn nodded enthusiastically again. "I wub peanut
butter cookies."

Marie had to smile. "Well then, peanut butter it is."

They'd no sooner creamed the butter and sugar together

when the back door opened. Marie turned around. It was Jason, scowling and stomping in high adolescent temper.

"What? What's the matter?"

"I didn't think it was possible. I mean, I really thought you were the absolute worst."

Marie closed her eyes. "What'd you do?"

"Nothing. All I did was—"

Marie shook her head. "Do you hear yourself, Jason? 'Nothing,' followed immediately by 'all I did was…'."

"Marie, the guy's a nutcase. So I missed a stop sign. It's not like there was anybody coming or anything. One little stop sign and he has a brain spasm. He's like mental or something."

"Uh-huh. You breeze right through a stop sign and *he's* mental."

"I knew you'd take his side. Adults always stick to-gether." Jason threw up his hands in disgust and rage at the inequities of life. He pointed his index finger at Marie. "Well, I'll tell you something. This is total bullcrap about me having to earn the privilege of driving. Driving is not a privilege, it's a right and I don't care what you, Luke, Dad or the state of Indiana has to say about it. I'm fifteen. That makes me old enough. I'm an adult. If I have to I'll take myself out driving, so you can put that in your col-lective pipes and smoke it."

"Over my dead body," Marie retorted but she was speaking to empty space. Jason was retreating to the second floor. Unfortunately she doubted it would take all that long for him to regroup and come back down for a return skir-mish. The back door opened once more as music began to blare.

"There you are. I was beginning to worry he'd run you over and left you lying out in the street somewhere." Luke did not have the looks of a happy camper.

"The kid's a menace on the road."

"How bad could it have been?" Marie asked and almost

laughed. She'd been out with Jason. She knew exactly how
bad it could be and just how fast driving with Jason could
reduce a person to a whimpering mass of twitching nerve
endings. "You weren't gone all that long."

"Felt like a lifetime." Luke dragged a hand through his
hair. "I think we got caught up in a male dominance kind
of thing. Jason was trying to establish himself as head wolf
and wasn't real happy with the end result of the contest."

"I assume I'm now talking to the leader of the pack?"

"Shut up," Luke said and ran the back of two fingers
down her cheek in a gesture he'd wanted to indulge since
he'd first seen her. He no longer felt the need to resist.
They were engaged, after all. If seeing Jason through to his
license was part of the package, then being able to reach
out and touch Marie's creamy skin whenever he felt like it
was the flip side, the compensation. He'd earned it.

Marie meant to keep the banter light. It was the only
way to survive life with Jason, but Luke's touch wiped the
smile right off her face. She looked up into his eyes. His
gaze was equally solemn. Her cheek tingled and in a non-
thinking gesture she reached up and trapped his hand
against her face.

"What'd he do?" she asked in an almost breathless
whisper as she stared up into his eyes. Wade's eyes, but
not Wade's. She studied them. They were the same color,
but that's where any similarities ended. Eyes were supposed
to be the window to the soul, but she'd never found herself
unable to break contact with Wade's eyes. Luke's were like
a bottomless well she could gaze into forever. "What'd he
do?" she repeated.

Luke gave in to temptation. He kissed her forehead. His
heart rate wasn't exactly calming down, but he much preferred this kind of cardiac stimulation, although, between
Jason's driving and Marie's proximity Luke figured he'd
be lucky if his heart made it another month before giving

out on him. "What didn't he do?" he replied, breaking the spell between them.

"I think he thought I'd be impressed by the amount of rubber he could lay down during his takeoffs and landings," Luke continues, "He almost took out a bicyclist before we'd even gotten two blocks away. If he wasn't on two wheels going around corners it wasn't for lack of trying and he'd have seen the stop sign if he hadn't been so busy checking out Mary Beth somebody or other who was sunbathing in a bikini on the roof of her front porch which was evidently just outside her bedroom window."

Marie sighed. In all truth, she wasn't surprised. "I've spoken to him about keeping his eyes on the road."

"It'll sink in once we've clashed a few more times."

Marie tipped her head back. "You're planning on going back out with him?"

It wasn't like he was looking forward to it. He'd like to live long enough to at least get Carolyn through kindergarten but he was a man of his word, damn it all. At times like this he wished there was a bit more of Wade in him. They'd been brothers, after all. "Did you think I'd bail out the moment the going got tough?"

Yes. Yes, she had. She'd been wrong and Marie blushed, feeling guilty. "It's not your problem, Luke."

"You shouldn't have to deal with it all on your own. Try to remember you're not alone anymore, Marie. Lean on me. I won't let you down. I'm strong. Together, presenting a united front, we'll be invincible."

It was a novel idea, someone to lean on. "Luke, he's threatening to take the car out by himself."

"Talk," Luke assured her.

Marie was doubtful. "I don't know. He was pretty angry at not being able to intimidate you."

"I promise you, he won't." He dipped his hand in his pocket and came out with—something unidentifiable but oily looking.

"What's—"

There was barely time to realize the music had stopped when they heard Jason's feet pounding down the carpeted stairs.

Luke's hand disappeared back into his pocket as Jason appeared in the kitchen doorway. He came through and snatched up the car keys from the countertop where Luke had returned them. Giving them both a defiant look he breezed out the back door before Marie could even issue a protest.

Marie made to go after him, Luke forestalled her with a hand on her arm. He shook his head at her. "Wait," he said. "He'll be back."

Sure enough there was no sound of an engine starting up.

"Did he change his mind?" Marie wondered out loud five minutes later. "He was so mad I thought for sure—"

Luke shook his head in a small negative movement. "He didn't change his mind."

"Then wh—"

The back door flew open in a movement so violent Marie expected it to fly right off the hinges. Jason came through the doorway, his face purple with impotent rage. He hurled the keys down and Carolyn stared up at him wide-eyed. "What?" Marie said.

"Make him fix it."

"Make who fix what?" Marie asked.

Jason pointed a finger at her. "Don't mess with me, Marie. I'm serious. He did something to the car so it wouldn't start. Make him fix it."

Luke rocked innocently on his heels and gave Marie a bland smile.

Marie looked doubtfully from Jason to Luke and back again. She smiled. The man was a genius. "Jason, in case you haven't noticed, Luke is twice as big as I am. How do you suggest I go about making him do something?"

Jason's face turned a deeper purple. "I mean it, Marie. I'm telling Dad if you don't. You know it's not good for him to be upset. You know—"

That did it. Jason's blatant manipulations were too reminiscent of his brother. "Why, you slimy little punk," Luke all but snarled. "Of all the self-centered—you sure know what buttons to push, don't you? Well, you're not taking out your temper on Marie. Or your father."

"Uh, Luke..."

"No. Call his bluff. Not even a fifteen-year-old who specializes in being egocentric would go through with what he's threatening. Call his bluff." Luke stood to his full height and moved closer so he was towering over Jason in as intimidating a manner as possible.

Marie tried to intervene one more time. "Maybe I'd better—"

"Call him, Jason. Call your dad." Luke gestured toward the back kitchen wall. "There's the telephone. Do it. Set your dad's recovery back, it's okay. What's important is that you get your way, isn't it? Well, isn't it?" Luke pushed relentlessly when Jason made no move toward the phone.

"It's four-thirty," Jason extemporized. "He's probably not in his room. He's probably getting therapy or something. I'll call him after dinner, don't think I won't."

Jason and Luke stared each other down. Marie wondered wildly if the same rule that applies to dogs—the one glancing away first was accepting the dominance of the other—applied here. Jason looked about ready to take a swing at Luke and good grief, Luke appeared to be hopeful. The testosterone levels in her grandfather's kitchen right then were quite probably off the top of the charts. "Um, Carolyn, maybe we should get back to our cookies—"

"You stay right here, Marie," Jason directed without looking away. "And you get this bozo off my back. The only reason he wants to marry you is so he'll have me to push around, I can see it all now. I'm smaller than he is and he needs somebody to lord it over. I knew he couldn't be seriously interested in you.''

Marie rolled her eyes at the veiled insult. ''Thanks a lot, Jase. You have a lot of faith in my ability to attract the opposite sex, don't you? Now let's see if I've got this right. You expect me to believe that a man, any man, would propose marriage to a woman, any woman, in order to gain a mannerless fifteen-year-old? Jason, that's ridiculous.''

''Marie—''

''No,'' Luke said and all conversation stopped. ''Marie, you and Carolyn go ahead and finish making your cookies. Jason is done using you for a verbal punching bag every time he gets upset.''

''Don't tell me—'' Jason began.

''You say you're a man,'' Luke interrupted curtly. ''Prove it. A real man learns to channel his anger. He doesn't take it out on an innocent woman. He doesn't traumatize young children and he doesn't dump it on his elderly father. He also doesn't kick puppies or abuse kittens. I'm not saying a real man doesn't feel anger, frustration or any other emotion, just that he knows how to properly channel his feelings in a nondestructive manner. He finds a bag to punch, fence post holes that need digging, nails that need hammering, weights that need lifting, a ball to bash up against a wall with a racquet. Some nondestructive way of blowing off steam.''

Marie stood there with her mouth hanging open while Jason sputtered. ''Marie,'' he finally said with a sad shake of his head. ''What the hell is he talking about?''

''Don't swear in front of the baby'' was all Marie could come back with.

''Come on,'' Luke directed. ''You've got a bench press downstairs?''

''No, I use a friend's,'' Jason said and smirked, pleased to shoot down Luke's plan, whatever it was.

''Fine, I've got one. And a good set of weights. We'll

go to my place. My guess is you can't do more than two sets of bicep curling reps. How much weight do you use?''

Jason's eyes narrowed as he calculated. He took a fifteen-year-old's great pride in his workout routine. ''For curling reps? Seventy-five pounds including the bar. Think you can top that, big guy?''

Luke took his keys out of his pocket. ''Let's go. I'll even spot you ten pounds.''

''You're not spotting me nothing, macho man. I don't need any favors from you. Hold on. I've got to go upstairs and get my gym shorts.''

Marie let Carolyn stir while she added an egg and vanilla to the cookie mixture. ''Luke, I don't want you to get carried away here—''

Luke looked insulted. ''I'm not going to get hurt. I work out. Believe me, Marie, I can outlast that little weasel.''

Marie was astonished by his conclusion. ''Well, of course you can outlast Jason. Look at you. Your shoulders are as broad as a barn door, for heaven's sake. You either buy your shirts too small or you've got biceps to die for.''

Luke felt an embarrassed blush start to bloom. Did she really think so? He'd never had his body discussed quite so frankly before. Men dissected women, he knew. Did women really talk like this about the men in their lives?

''The best part is, you've still got a neck. Here, honey. Let's add the flour now. Stir very gently.''

''A neck?''

''Yeah,'' Marie said trying to sound matter-of-fact. ''A neck. You ever really look at some of those professional football players or wrestlers? Some of the bodybuilders? They build themselves up so much they lose their neck. They couldn't do up their top shirt button if their life depended on it. They'd need about a size thirty neck to do it. It's gross.''

Luke had always thought so. He'd designed his workouts to find a happy medium and he'd never touched a steroid.

Not even in late adolescence when he'd gained his adult height but was still waiting to fill out. He'd never expected a woman to notice, however. In fact, there had been times when he'd felt like they'd gladly trample over him in the weight room to get to the more serious steroid-city types. Truth was, he had a hard time believing this.

"Wade had no neck," Luke pointed out suspiciously. Wade had also been heavily into steroids. "You were certainly attracted to him. You married him."

Marie dismissed that with a flick of her hand. "I was also seventeen years old when I met him. My first boyfriend. My only boyfriend. What did I know? Heck, I thought the vinegar they pass off as red wine was the wine of choice for sophisticated drinkers back then." She made it sound like a million years ago. "I like to think I've matured since then."

Luke studied her thoughtfully for a minute. "I'll leave you Carolyn's car seat. Bring her home when you're ready. We'll order out Chinese."

It was hard not to bristle. Couldn't the man ever ask? Real men might not eat quiche but they had manners, didn't they? For a minute or two, she'd felt close to Luke. Her stomach was thinking about acting up again, however, and she just didn't have the energy to argue. "Whatever," Marie agreed tiredly and turned back to her half-finished dough.

Jason stomped down the stairs, and he and Luke left after arranging to rendezvous once the cookies were baked. When she was alone again with Carolyn, Marie pondered the scene that had just taken place.

"Real men felt anger, but they knew how to channel it in nondestructive ways," she repeated to herself as she helped Carolyn plop spoonfuls of dough down.

"Hmm." It was a new concept. Wade had put his fist through more than one door or wall when he'd lost his temper. And while Wade had never used his hands on her, his tongue had been another matter. He'd had the *appearance* of manliness, but—hmm.

And if a real man could feel anger, how about the other emotions? For example, could he learn to love? And how about a widow pregnant with his brother's child who came equipped with an obnoxious fifteen-year-old and an ailing grandparent? Could he learn to love her?

"Hmm."

Chapter Nine

Jason and Luke worked out together and each impressed the other. In between reps they developed a male locker room sort of respect and rapport. "You on any of the teams at school?" Luke asked as they did side-by-side crunches.

"Nah," Jason answered, breathless but gamely straining to keep up. "I was the last cut from the frosh basketball team last year, wrestling's not my thing and you were probably a football jock like your brother, but the coach at Saint Joe Valley is like, stupid or something. I mean, he's got players with bad knees and he gets the trainer to shoot them up with cortisone and sends them out to play some more. He doesn't care if they're left with a bad joint for the rest of their lives, he just wants another Indiana High School Athletic Association trophy for the hall trophy case. And you should hear some of the stuff he says to the guys." Jason rolled his eyes. "Mr. Macho. Kind of guy who makes you believe in evolution, you know?"

"Yeah." Luke knew. He'd had enough contact with high school coaches during his own high school career. He knew.

"Man, how many of these things are we going to do? We passed two hundred a while back."

Luke was surprised to hear that. But then, he had his own frustrations he was trying to work out. For God's sake, he'd just proposed marriage to the niece of the juvenile delinquent beside him. Not only that, but said niece was pregnant with another man's child and had an amorous grandfather in need of rehabilitation he'd also be responsible for. Luke had no sooner left the Fort kitchen when he'd decided he was in dire need of serious introspection, self-evaluation and, quite possibly, psychiatric counseling. It was glaringly apparent to him he had a death wish of some kind of other. He needed to make out a will. Leave the whole kit and kaboodle to some other poor unsuspecting slob, then kill himself. Let's see, who did he hate the most?

"Luke?"

"Hmm? Oh, right. I guess we can be done with abs." He flipped onto his stomach and began push-ups. He put one arm behind his back. "You ever try one-handed?"

Jason groaned, shook his head and good-naturedly stuck a hand behind his back. "You're nuts, man, you know that? I suppose you were a superjock like your brother. Probably really got into that no-neck football mentality, huh?"

"Nah, I knew I was going to major in business and would have to button a shirt. I left the steroids to Wade. I swam. Made it to states junior and senior year. Butterfly and a couple of relays. Our medley had the school pool record for a while. Probably long gone now."

"No joke? I can just see you parading around in one of those little Speedos."

"Hey, the girls on the team didn't seem to object."

Jason snorted. "I did some age group swimming. Up until seventh grade as a matter of fact."

Luke switched to his other hand and Jason followed suit. "You any good at it?"

"Not really. Just okay. And the chlorine turned my hair green."

He had a blinding flash of inspiration. "Saturate your hair with tap water and wear a cap. That'll keep your hair from turning colors. You ought to think about getting back to it," Luke casually suggested. Actually, he'd see to it. Unless things had changed drastically, when swimmers were in season they got up at four-thirty in the morning and swam a couple of hours before school then returned immediately after school for another few hours. Swimmers were generally too tired to get into trouble. There was no time and no energy to sink into the swamp of hormone hell where other adolescents their age dwelt. Yes, he'd see to it that Jason got back in the water. It could easily be the cure for one of Marie's problems. Not only would Jason be clean after being pickled in chlorine for several hours per day, he'd also be too tired to be obnoxious. In fact, Jason would probably end up sharing Carolyn's eight-thirty bedtime.

Good thinking, Luke, he congratulated himself, using both hands now to do his push-ups. That would leave Marie and Luke by themselves in front of the fireplace once they'd married—at least until Ray Fort came home from the nursing home. He could see it all now. Marie, wearing something sexy, something filmy but not transparent. Those auburn curls of hers would glint red in the firelight as she reclined on the carpet in front of the fire.

Unconsciously, Luke licked his lips. Naturally there'd be champagne. A decent label, too, nothing cheap. Music. Something seductive, um, *Bolero*. No, too short. He wanted more time than that. There'd be nothing rushed when he slowly convinced her to lose the negligee or whatever it was they called those filmy things women used to drive men out of their minds. Would Marie even own something like that? Luke paused to consider the problem. Nothing in the wardrobe he'd seen so far indicated she'd go in for the punch-in-the-gut type night wear.

He'd buy her one as a wedding present. Better to be safe than sorry, he always said. Pleased with his solution, Luke continued to paint his mental picture.

Once Luke had her naked maybe he'd anoint her breasts with the champagne. Then lick it off. He'd never seen her naked of course, but unless her bosom came off with her bra, Marie was stacked. Luke decided to be positive. They'd be full. And pale. Maybe there'd be just a trace of blue vein showing beneath the skin. Her nipples would be enlarged by her pregnancy. They'd be pink. No, dusty rose. No, wait. Champagne-colored but with a blush, that was it. His push-ups picked up speed as he pictured the scene. Who the hell cared what color her nipples were? They'd be his. His to lick, to suck, to nip. Luke swallowed.

Luke knew he should stop torturing himself, but the mental movie reel just wouldn't stop rolling. Before Luke knew it, he saw himself spilling a bit of the bubbly into her navel, dipping his tongue in, sipping and—

"Damn," he muttered, shaking his head in rueful amusement at himself. Here he was, virtually totally exhausted and still, his fantasy involving Marie was strong enough to bring his lower body achingly alive.

"What?" Jason breathlessly inquired.

"Nothing." Luke lowered himself gingerly onto the workout mat, cautiously reaching down and adjusting himself before collapsing. Face buried in his arm, he breathed deeply, willing his body back under his control.

Jason simply groaned and collapsed. "Man, I give up. You win. I'm dead. You can fix whatever you did to the car. I'm not going anywhere. Not for a month of Sundays."

Luke reached over and punched the younger man on the shoulder in a male's recognition of acceptance but he felt no real sense of victory. Luke might now be the official leader of the pack in Jason's eyes, but where was he supposed to be leading them and how was he to get them there?

He shook his head, groaned and slowly rose. Once on his feet, he gave Jason a hand up. And he still had to deal with Carolyn's dinner, bath, bedtime stories, prayers, sweeping the monsters out from the closet and under the bed. God.

He slapped Jason on the back in a comradely gesture understood only by men and they started up the basement stairs. One day at a time, Luke told himself. One day at a time.

Marie arrived shortly thereafter with an aluminum pie plate overloaded with peanut butter cookies. She found Jason and Luke totally at ease with each other, all harsh words forgotten while they discussed and experimented with the ins and outs of Luke's surround sound system.

"I will never understand the male mind," she informed Carolyn as she transferred the cookies to a plate. "They are a complete and utter enigma," she announced, "and probably really do come from Mars."

Carolyn merely giggled and filched herself another cookie. "Good," she said.

Marie smiled and ruffled her hair. "That's the last one," she told the child for easily the third time. "This time I mean it. The absolute last."

Carolyn smiled engagingly, cookie crumbs stuck in her teeth. "Milk, pease," she said.

"Okay," Marie agreed. "At least that's good for you." She poured the toddler an inch in the bottom of a cup. "There you go."

She ought to collect Jason and leave, that's what she should do. She needed time to think, time to consider. Was she really going to marry Luke? She'd made one bad mistake, was she compounding the error or correcting it?

"Who knows?" she asked herself, throwing up her arms in frustration. "Who the heck knows?"

"Now this is what the subwoofer—"

Marie shook her head, turned around and went back to

the kitchen. Subwoofers and their attendant paraphernalia, remote controls and Monday night football were, Marie was willing to hazard a guess, single-handedly responsible for the soaring divorce rate and the downfall of the institution of marriage. Some sociologist should do a study. "Boys with toys," she sighed and proceeded to go through Luke's refrigerator and cupboards in search of anything edible. Luke had offered to order out but he seemed too involved to bother.

She found a package of chicken parts that had bled all over the refrigerator shelf but was still within code, half a box of Bisquick and an onion that hadn't sprouted too badly. "It'll do," she muttered through pursed lips and went back to the refrigerator. Hadn't she seen— "Ah, there you are. You can't hide from me." Marie added a plastic squeezie lemon that didn't feel totally empty to her hoard.

"Spices, spices, who's got the spices?" She opened one door after another, finally hitting pay dirt. "Here we go. I suppose it's too much to ask for a little rosemary. Vanilla, pepper, yeah, yeah, let's see. Chili powder, good grief, this has never even been opened. Neither has this." Marie shook her head. "Aha! Rosemary." That can was also still sealed. "Very strange."

Maybe she should check with Luke before she just took over. He might really want to order Chinese. Then again, it was five-thirty. Carolyn needed to be fed. Marie stuck her head in the family room doorway.

"Listen to this," she heard. "Stadium sound." She saw Luke gesture toward the wide-screen TV. "Pretty good, hunh? Perfect for Monday night football, Pacer games, whatever."

"That is totally fat," Jason said and Marie assumed he was concurring.

Luke pushed a button. "Here's small theater…large theater…"

It was obvious to Marie that Luke and Jason were lost

in some sort of temporal boy toy time warp. Who knew when they'd return to the real world?

"I'm making the fricassee and to heck with it," she decided. "Carolyn needs to eat and I can have it ready long before either one of them surfaces." She proceeded to flour and brown the chicken pieces she'd found. It wasn't long before the heavenly scent of onion and browning poultry permeated the room. Luke, with Jason close behind, entered the kitchen sniffing the air like puppies hot on a trail.

"Something smells awfully good," Luke said.

Marie noticed he watched intently her every step just as he had the night she'd made the sloppy joes.

"What have you done so far?"

She looked at him oddly. "Nothing terribly exciting. I dipped the chicken into a mixture of flour, salt, pepper and paprika. Now I'm sautéing it with some onions. Why? What are you, the kitchen cop?"

He shrugged. "Jason, set the table," Luke directed without taking his attention off her. It was difficult not to squirm under his intense regard. "Plates are up above next to where you're standing. Get Carolyn to help you count, okay? Watch her threes. Sometimes she likes to skip them. What're you going to do next?"

"I'm going to add water, a squirt of lemon juice and a little rosemary."

"That it?"

"No, that's not it. Then I'm going to get wild and crazy and add dumplings. Luke, what is it with you and my cooking? I haven't killed anybody yet if that's what you're worried about."

Luke ignored her. "How much?"

"For crying out loud," Marie said as she dumped a glass of water over the mixture. It sizzled nicely and released a fragrant cloud of steam. "How much what?"

Luke's eyes narrowed as he tried to compute the capacity of the glass she'd used. "Water, to start."

"I don't know. Half a cup. A cup."

"Well, which is it?"

"Luke, I don't know. Jason's mom taught me how to cook. She was an old-time cook who never measured anything. She just eyeballed it." Marie sprinkled some rosemary on top of the brew. "You add water until you've got enough. You put a pinch of spice in, taste it and add more if you need to. A squirt of lemon juice." She demonstrated. "I don't know. Honest. It's not a trick. I just do it."

Luke stuck his hands in his pocket and scowled. "Fat lot of good that is."

"Sorry. I'll never cook for you again."

Luke scowled. "Don't be ridiculous. Just pay attention to what you're doing."

"I am paying attention. See? Watch me pay attention while I add water and parsley to the Bisquick."

"Very funny. At least the directions for that are on the side of the box." Luke watched in silence for a moment, intent on exactly how Marie went about plopping spoonfuls of dough into the mixture on the stove top. The damn irritating woman seemed to have no system at all. She just used a regular spoon out of the drawer and appeared to willy-nilly drop blobs wherever the spirit moved her. His scowl deepened.

"Your frown is going to curdle the broth," Marie warned as she reached to set the timer for the dumplings. "Why don't you go help Jason and Carolyn? I need to get some green beans going here and you're definitely in the way."

"It's my kitchen," Luke reminded her, refusing to budge.

"Oh, for...here." She handed him a pot. "Put some water in here to boil the vegetables."

"How much water?" Luke asked with exaggerated patience.

"Enough to cover the bottom of the pan with a little to spare!"

"There's no need to yell," Luke admonished.

"Ahh!"

"Man, for a duo about to be hitched, you two don't seem all that lovey-dovey, you know? Quit yelling at each other. You're gonna upset the little peanut princess here. We've counted everything in sight, man, and all I gotta say is math isn't exactly the little peanut's strong suit. We haven't made it successfully to five yet, let alone ten."

"Don't be sexist," Marie snapped. "Girls can do math, too. We'll work with her, that's all. Did you put napkins around?"

Jason looked at her blankly. "What for?"

"What...never mind. Forget it. I give up."

Jason looked to Luke. "What's her problem?"

The timer dinged. Marie thought about hitting Jason over the head with the pan of chicken fricassee but figured Carolyn shouldn't be exposed to violence. Instead she slapped a hot pad on the tabletop, lifted the heavy pan and prepared to bring it over to the table.

Luke was up in a second, staying her hand. "What are you doing?"

It was a shame to waste a body like that on an unbalanced mind, but it was the only excuse she could think of. First there was the inspection of each and every ingredient, including exact quantities, like it made a difference whether it had been a teaspoon of rosemary or three-quarters of a teaspoon—what had the man majored in during college, anal retentiveness? Now this.

"Putting supper on the table. What's it look like I'm doing?"

Luke forced her hand back down, then took the pan himself. "You shouldn't be lifting that. I'll do it."

Her jaw dropped. "Excuse me? I'm not capable of lifting a pan of chicken?"

"That's right." He looked around and directed Jason, "You two go wash your hands for supper. Give her a hand, will you, Jason?"

"What for? We're using forks and stuff, aren't we? I mean, it's not like I'm planning on using my fingers or anything."

"Jason," Marie said with a long-suffering sigh, "just go wash your hands." When he was out of hearing Marie smiled apologetically. "He's just giving you a hard time. The kid showers three times a day. Ordinarily he takes cleanliness to an extreme."

Jason could eat with his toes for all Luke cared. "You feeling okay?"

Marie wished he hadn't asked. She'd been feeling fine until she'd thought about it. She touched her flat stomach, still unable to believe a life was growing there. "Now that you mention it, no. Not really."

"Here, you sit down," Luke said, all solicitous as he guided her back to the table. "I'll take over now. You did the hard part. I can handle the serving."

Jason looked at him as though Luke had suddenly grown horns and Marie was fairly shocked herself. In her experience, men didn't offer to do menial jobs. Her grandfather was of a different generation, Jason and Wade were just plain jerks.

She leaned back in her chair, closed her eyes and listened. Marie could hear the scrape of the spoon against the cast-iron skillet she'd used. Luke must have served Carolyn first because he was now directing Jason to mush the little one's food while he finished filling plates. Suddenly the smells that had been so heavenly a short while ago were much closer, virtually right under her nose, and Marie knew her plate had been filled. She opened her eyes. Jason had his knife in his right hand, his fork in his left. He cut his chicken, then shoveled it into his mouth. She supposed she ought to be grateful he hadn't picked it up in his bare hands.

"Jason, you cut, then you set the knife down and transfer your fork to your right hand before you eat with it."

"That's stupid."

"It's good manners. You continue to eat like that and nobody'll date you let alone marry you."

Jason shrugged and Marie knew she was in for needling. "So? I'll wait for Miss Oink Oink to grow up," he said, indicating Carolyn with a wave of his laden fork. "Look at her. She's using her fingers. I'm a suave sophisticate next to her. It's a waste of time to be switching hands all the time."

Marie had to bite her lip to keep from laughing at the mental image of Carolyn toddling down the aisle in a wedding gown to meet smart-aleck Jason at the altar. Then her mind began playing tricks and suddenly it was Marie meeting Luke and the humor was gone. Luke would be devastating in a tux and how Marie wished she could be the blushing virginal bride all done up in white with a long train and veil for him instead of the casual ceremony they'd be bound to have. The image shattered when Luke leaned forward and began to lecture.

"It may seem like a waste of effort and time and Carolyn may be using her fingers now but as she observes the world around her, she is implanting archetypal images on her subconscious on relationships and behavior patterns in the real world. It's important we set a good example so she has good images that will allow her to operate in the real world as a functional, contributing adult."

Jason stared at him, then turned to Marie. "What'd he just say?"

"Switch hands and use your fork correctly."

"Got it."

"And put a napkin in your lap unless you want to hear it all over again."

"Right."

And he did it. That was the amazing part. Marie was so

surprised she forgot about how ill she was feeling and took a bite of dumpling. The bread seemed to settle her stomach. She finished the dumpling, ate a small amount of chicken and even got a few green beans down. Luke set a glass of milk in front of her.

"Drink," he commanded.

Marie sighed but upended the glass. It would take too much precious energy to argue.

Luke nodded, pleased. He rose and began clearing the table. "Jason, grab the rest of the stuff, will you?"

Jason looked ready to argue, then glanced at Carolyn. "I told you, she could marry me," he tried in a relatively feeble attempt for him.

"Carolyn is not going to grow up to wait on some man. She's going to medical or law school and her time will be far too valuable. You know, every time Bill Gates stops and ties his shoes it costs him a couple of mill. As a matter of fact—"

Jason raised his hands in defeat. "I'll do it." And he rose and started to clear. "But I'll tell you this much, when she's a doctor I am not going to her for medical help. Kid can't even count to five without messing up. No way I am letting her loose on my body for anything more complicated than a hangnail check."

Luke shrugged. "Your loss. Marie and I got her some of those cardboard sewing cards with pictures on them yesterday afternoon and she did really well. Only messed up a couple of holes. I was thinking maybe a surgeon."

Marie had to grin. Luke was really getting into this fatherhood thing. She touched her stomach and got a dreamy look on her face. What about her own baby? If she had a son, there could be no better role model than Luke. He was everything a man should be. Maybe her son could grow up to be president. No, who in their right mind would want that for their child? A lawyer or a surgeon with Carolyn as mentor would be better. She hated to be sexist, but prima ballerina or professional princess might not be bad occupations for a daughter either.

Marie laughed out loud at that and picked up Carolyn, ready to lug her to the sink for a wash up.

Luke was immediately there. "Here, I'll do that." And very efficiently, he did. He took the toddler into the family room and put on a Disney film with the surround sound on large theater and the subwoofer way up. It didn't matter that it wasn't a rock band, Jason was so impressed by the booming bass that he joined Carolyn for the movie.

Marie peeked in on them after helping Luke right the kitchen, and smiled tenderly. There was hope for Jason after all. Carolyn had climbed into his lap and had her head resting against his chest while she sucked her thumb.

"Hey, come on, peanut," Jason was saying, "you've got to watch this part. It's not that scary. I've got you, don't I? Man, this babe is the Queen of Evil, huh? She is raw. But you don't have to worry. The mommy and daddy dogs are going to save all one hundred and one puppies before Her Evilness can make a coat out of them. Promise."

Carolyn sucked harder and Jason's arm came around her and he actually squeezed in a comforting gesture. Marie was amazed.

"Hey, listen," Jason continued, unaware he was being observed. "I didn't mean to screw you up by saying one hundred and one, okay? Technically you're only supposed to say 'and' for a decimal point. I should have said one hundred one, okay? So, like, when you're forming those subconscious mathematical arche-whatevers Luke was talking about remember to save the 'ands' for decimal points. One hundred one *and* no tenths puppies, got it?"

Jason had missed the point of Luke's monologue, but watching him interact with Carolyn was still sweet. Marie turned around and rejoined Luke in the kitchen.

"He's so cute with her," she said. "When he thinks nobody's looking, he's really a nice kid."

Luke set a cup of herbal tea in front of her. "Yeah, if we live through it I think he's going to be fine." He sat across from her with a steaming mug of coffee. "I made instant," he said. "But if the smell still bothers you I'll toss it."

Marie, who'd been about to take a sip, paused. Maybe it was stupid, but she was touched. Offering to pour out a cup of coffee might not seem like much, but for the past several years it was the nicest thing anybody had ever done for her. Right then, Luke Deforest seemed the perfect man. A beautifully wrapped package with an actual present inside, not an empty box.

When Luke was away from Marie, he felt trapped. As soon as she was in the room, it was all he could do to keep his hands to himself. For the first time in Luke's life he felt victimized by his hormones. Even as an adolescent he'd had better control. It just didn't matter that Marie was pregnant with somebody else's baby. He wanted her. Badly. Irrevocably. Luke took a healthy swig of coffee, singeing his tongue.

Marie sat with Luke at the kitchen table, sipping her tea and nibbling the graham crackers he'd set out. It was quiet, but the silence was companionable. In the background the dishwasher softly sloshed, the bug light next door relentlessly zapped while in the family room puppies were relentlessly chased on the screen. Life went on all around them but the kitchen table was their own private oasis. A sense of peacefulness permeated her. Muscles she hadn't even known were tense began to relax.

"Wouldn't it be neat if every now and then you could just take off for a deserted island?" Marie asked, stretching her arms up over her head and bending side to side. "You know, your own private hideaway where you could just sit for a while, sort of vegetate while you recharged your batteries?"

Luke stared at her thoughtfully. "You work so hard, always giving, you could probably use some time to simply collapse, couldn't you? Especially now with the toll the pregnancy is taking on your body. You've got to be exhausted.''

Marie rose and carried her cup to the sink. "I have to admit I'm pretty tired right now. I don't think of my life as all that stressful. I quit my job when I moved home and there hasn't been time to find another one so it's not like I've also had to juggle work and home both like some women, but between Grandpa and Jason I guess I've been pretty wired.''

Luke came up behind her, reaching around her to set his own mug in the sink. He rested his hands on her shoulders and lightly massaged.

"Oh," Marie moaned. "That feels good.''

He dug deeper and Marie all but wilted in his arms.

"I've been doing some reading," Luke said. God, it felt good to finally have his hands on her.

"God help us," Marie responded. "On what now?''

"Pregnancy. Found an article in one of the child care magazines I picked up. Read it late last night.''

"Yeah? What'd it say? I haven't had time to do much research yet.'' Marie tilted her head forward to give him better access.

"For one thing, the fatigue thing is totally normal.'' He continued to rub but it became more of a caress. She had the softest skin.

Marie shivered.

"So's the nausea. But it'll pass.'' It wasn't something he'd planned, but it was hardly his fault her neck was so darned tempting. He kissed Marie's nape.

"Glad to hear it.'' she murmured, no longer quite so relaxed. Luke's warmth radiated into her back and she suddenly realized how close he was. She was virtually trapped between the sink and Luke's much larger, more powerful body. "Uh, what else did it say?" she asked a bit breathlessly.

His large hands paused, then he slowly moved them over her shoulders and down onto her upper chest. "It says your breasts will probably feel tender." He tenderly massaged the upper slopes then slipped his hands underneath to support them. "So...are they?"

"Yes," she all but whispered, grateful any sound at all had come out. She was having a slight problem getting air in. He was really crowding her now.

Luke kissed her neck once more. "Am I hurting you? Is this too much?"

"Ah, no." Marie took a deep breath. "Actually, it, um, feels pretty good."

"Yeah?" he whispered seductively, the front of his whole body snuggled right up against her backside now.

She cleared her throat. "Yeah."

He skimmed her nipples. "How about this?"

Marie jumped. "Oh, my." Fascinated, eyes wide, she watched his hands hover over the peaks of her breasts.

"Good or too much?"

"Do it again," she urged and he did. Collapsing back against him she captured his hands and pressed them lightly against herself. "More."

She was killing him. Luke laughed a bit roughly but obliged. Gently Luke rubbed and massaged her tender nipples.

Marie leaned against him and closed her eyes as pleasure overwhelmed her. She concentrated on the sensations he evoked, very much on sensory overload and enjoying every bit of it. "They've been so sore, Luke," she confessed. "I can't even describe how good...oh! What are you doing to them? To me? Oh!" Marie began writhing against him. "I don't believe this. I think I'm going to...oh! Stop! Luke, you've got to stop."

But Luke was too fascinated watching her electric re-

sponse to his gentle stimuli and he continued to skim his
hand over her nipples. Then he began gently pulling them.

And Marie went over the edge.

Amazed, Luke continued the light pressure and watched
while Marie shivered and shook in his arms. When she
finally collapsed, he carefully supported her.

"Holy cow," he said reverently, unable to believe what
he'd just witnessed.

Marie was mortified. Never in her life... "Um—"

Luke immediately stopped her. "No, don't say anything
to spoil it. That was one of the most beautiful things I've
ever seen. Have you ever—no, don't tell me. I'm just going
to let myself think it was me and my incredible technique.
Lady, you are *hot!*"

Marie sagged against him, closing her eyes as her face
burned. Great. Now he probably thought she was some kind
of bimbo sex fiend. Wonderful.

"How are they now?" Luke asked, all solicitous. Man
alive, he'd like to see that again. It made him feel strong,
virile. She'd been putty in his hands. Damn.

Marie had other ideas. "Fine. Much better."

He pressed, not quite willing to give up just yet. She'd
gone up like a firecracker. No one had ever responded to
him like that. This was no mere woman he had in his hands.
"Not all the way better?"

"Well, no. I imagine they'll be a bit sensitive from now
on. Didn't the article say?"

He could only hope. "Want me to do it some more?"

"Ah, no. That's okay." She didn't even want to know
if he could make her do that again. It gave Luke too much
power. "I really need to take Jason and get going. Tomorrow's a school day."

"Oh, yeah, right." Luke reluctantly stepped back and
jammed his hands into his jeans pockets. "I'm going to
call the high school tomorrow and check into the swim
team for him."

"I can do it."

Luke scowled. "I want to."

"Well, all right, then. I'll just...go then. Ah, thanks for everything."

Luke shrugged away her gratitude. "No problem. I'll call you tomorrow."

"All right. Well, then...see you, I guess." And she all but fled the scene.

Later, after Luke put Carolyn to bed, he lay on top of the sheets of his own bed, his hands behind his head, thinking. He was a man who liked to be in control, captain of his ship, so to speak. His life hadn't been bothering to consult with him overly much lately, careening on its merry way and leaving him to constantly try to catch up. He'd been resentful. And for what? Fate could be a beautiful thing. Look what it had sent him. Carolyn, who was really growing on him. The little one filled a hole he hadn't even known existed. And Marie. True, she came with baggage but it was a fee he was willing to pay. He'd never met another woman so warm and giving.

The personality of a saint.

And the body to tempt one.

Chapter Ten

Marie went to sleep that night feeling like a stranger in her own body. She woke up feeling pretty much the same way. More than any other time in her life, she regretted the lack of a close female friend. She had no one to confide in. Her grandfather had always been her confidant for as long as she could remember. Marie could hardly talk to *him* about—she eyed her chest in the bathroom mirror—*this.*

She wandered restlessly around the house for a while, picking up a book here and setting it down over there, and accomplished virtually nothing. Finally, Marie swore, disgusted with herself. "This is ridiculous. One little orgasm and my brain is fried." Marie threw up her hands. "I need to get out of here. Take a drive. Clear the cobwebs out." So she got in the car and ended up driving to the nursing home.

In her own little world, her mind still mush, Marie had entered her grandfather's room before she realized he wasn't alone.

"Betty," she said, stopping in her tracks.

"Marie!"

She was greeted simultaneously by Luke's aunt and her grandfather. Marie watched as Betty pulled her hand away from her grandfather's and blushed. Marie hadn't even known people that old *could* blush. If she'd thought about it at all, she'd have assumed it was one of those functions the body lost as it aged. But here the two of them were...red. Marie shook her head in amazement. The experience was doing nothing to help clear up her sorry mental functions.

"Sorry. Didn't mean to interrupt."

"Don't be silly—"

"You didn't—"

"I can come back later. When it's more convenient. I mean—"

Ray finally took control. If Marie hadn't been so confused, she'd have been pleased to see his old crusty personality operating again. "Come back here, girl. I'm not dead from the waist down. Never have been. Good grief, I've worn out two women already, loved them both with everything in me. Hopefully I've still a ways to go before I give up on the opposite sex. So what?"

"I never thought—"

"Sure you did. Everybody thinks their parents and grandparents are eunuchs. We're all secretly convinced we're adopted. Either that or our parents had sex one time with their eyes closed and in the dark just so they could conceive us and fulfill themselves by having such a wonderful child."

Marie had to laugh. That was her grandfather. Outrageous and irreverent.

"Grandpa, you shouldn't talk like that in front of me."

"Bosh. An old married lady like you? You probably know more than I do."

As an adolescent, Marie had firmly believed that. She had her doubts now.

"I need to get back on the floor," Betty said. Marie watched her squeeze her grandfather's hand before bustling out the door. She backed up, giving Betty plenty of room. Then she came and sat by her grandfather's bedside.

"What is going on with you two?" she asked.

"Nothing," her grandfather replied innocently. "Yet."

Marie shook her head. "Holy smoke."

Ray wiggled his eyebrows at her. "Where there's smoke there's fire. I hope."

"Grandpa, you're incorrigible."

He sighed contentedly. "That's me."

Marie stared at him. "Grandpa, what's come over you? You're your old self again. What's happened since yesterday?"

"I've realized my life doesn't have to be over, that's what's happened. I was wallowing in self-pity, much as I hate to admit it. I may never be as limber as I was, kiddo. Hell, who am I kidding? I'll never be the same man I was fifteen, twenty years ago. Even five years ago. I felt useless, used up. Betty kept pushing and it made me madder than hell. Woman's got gumption. Doesn't back away from a bit of temper. Staying power. I like that in a woman. Anyway, you and your young man did your part to help me open my eyes yesterday and then Jason called last night."

"He did?" Marie was amazed.

"He calls almost every night. I don't think anyone's supposed to know."

"Why not?"

"I'm not saying it doesn't hurt that he won't come and see his own father," Ray cautioned, "but I'm trying to be understanding. Admitting he cares goes against his teenage-alienated-from-the-world-in-general-the-older-generation-in-particular macho image, I think. At any rate, we had a long talk. He's decided to go out for swim team. Your young man suggested it."

"Really?"

"Yeah. Should be good for him. Keep him tired. You know what?"

"No, what?"

"I realized that if I'm going to go to his meets I've got to get back on my feet. Dumb as it sounds, I've suddenly realized that I've got a few good years left in me."

"Of course you do," Marie declared loyally. "More than a few."

"Maybe, maybe not. But I'm sure of this much. I'm coming home to make your life miserable again, Marie."

She snorted her disbelief. "As if you could."

"I'm serious. And I'm going to live those years, not just put in time."

"Good for you."

"You may not think so after you hear what I want you to do. Now here's a list of the things I'll need..."

Marie left the nursing home a while later still in shock, her mind reeling. Her grandfather was going courting. He wanted flowers, chocolates and, since restaurants were out for a while, a picnic basket with a gourmet type meal so he could wine and dine on-site.

Marie, who'd still been thinking in terms of desert islands since her chance remark of the night before, had suggested a desert island effect to her grandfather as a sort of theme. He was stuck there in that room for a while. Why not pretend he was marooned?

"With Betty?" he'd asked.

"Why not?" she'd answered with a shrug. "I could maybe order a lei instead of cut flowers." He'd gone for it. A stop at a paper party goods store was now also on her agenda. Marie remembered seeing paper-accordion pleated palm trees there. The perfect touch, in her estimation, for their dinner. Her grandfather had thought of a camping lantern rather than the overhead ceiling fixture, and piña colada mix. He'd felt a coconut milk and pineapple juice based drink was a necessity.

Marie shook her head as she trotted down the sidewalk intent on her errands. Good grief. Her grandfather was a romantic. She'd lived almost her whole life with him and she'd never really known him. There were none so blind as those who would not see, she guessed.

The next few weeks went by in a blur. Luke gave Marie a diamond ring. The stone nestled between an emerald and a deeply colored amethyst, their birthstones. Marie had barely avoided crying, she'd been so touched.

Ray came home, not to his house, but to Luke's first-floor guest bedroom. Marie and Jason also moved in while Ray finished recovering. Ray slowly regained mobility. Betty might as well have come with them, she visited that frequently. Marie watched her seventy-year-old grandfather hold hands with a blushing woman who virtually matched him in size and weight. Marie knew he stole kisses whenever they thought no one was looking. He had Marie pick up some things for him from home. A book of poetry. A collection of George Winston romantic mood music tapes. His good robe. Marie rolled her eyes at that one and tried not to think of her grandfather and Betty in dishabille.

Jason joined the swim team. He wasn't that good but by the same token, as he built up his endurance the kid was surprisingly un-terrible. Not the best, but not the worst, either. He was still surly most of the time but he was too tired for his barbs to carry much bite or be delivered with any real conviction. Boys from the team started calling. Girl from the team began calling. Jason was fitting in.

Marie watched Carolyn during the day and Luke went back to work. Marie noticed how much more comfortable Luke was with Carolyn and vice versa. He read her bedtime stories, oversaw prayers and swept out monsters. On the weekends, Luke and Carolyn fussed around in the kitchen together, creating supper for the whole crew. First fish sticks and applesauce out of a jar. An actual meat loaf.

Then came the pièce de résistance, a pot roast that was even good.

Marie began to feel superfluous in her own life.

It was not a good feeling.

"At least the baby will need me," she assured herself. "For sure nobody else seems to." Everybody needed to be needed. Didn't anyone else understand that?

Her stomach was better. She kept soda crackers by her bed. Her solitary bed. Luke hadn't been really pushing her for a wedding date, even though he'd given her the beautiful ring. Had he changed his mind? She didn't know and she wasn't comfortable enough to bring it up herself. Marie was stressed, no doubt about it, but eating two crackers before she got up at least helped settle her stomach a lot. At any rate, the smells of dinner no longer upset her. Brewing coffee still about killed her. "Babycakes does *not* like that foul brew," she decided.

Marie was still tired a lot and tended to nap when Carolyn did. She lost her waistline, was developing a tummy and began to feel decidedly unattractive. Luke touched her a lot. He had Carolyn by the hand and Marie by the arm when they went walking in the evening. With Carolyn, Marie knew it was protective—to keep her from dashing into the street or falling. What was it with her?

Luke would come up behind her and knead her shoulders at odd moments. Usually when she was entertaining Carolyn. Finger painting at the kitchen table. Helping her dress up in a costume tutu and put on a show. What was that, gratitude or something more? On the surface it didn't seem sexual. There was certainly no repeat of the episode in the kitchen, more was the pity. Marie had never felt anything quite so intense as that in her life.

She'd tried to duplicate it herself when Luke showed no inclination.

It hadn't worked.

Luke's hands, Luke's touch, seemed to be an essential ingredient.

Did the man want her or not?

It seemed to Marie that she appeared to be eminently resistible. Not exactly every woman's goal in life. She didn't really want to be his buddy and she for sure didn't want to be his duty.

"Well, fine," Marie muttered to herself one day as she scraped the last bit of dough from the sides of a bowl in an attempt to gather up enough for one last cookie. "He doesn't need me? I don't need him. He doesn't want me? I don't... Well never mind that." Marie had never lied well, not even to herself. "I can do without him. I can do without anybody."

Using her finger, she cleaned the spoon then shoved the tray into the oven and set the timer. There would be warm cookies and cold milk when Carolyn woke up. Marie made her decision there and then. "When Grandpa and Jason move out I'm going, too."

Marie's brow wrinkled. The night before, after Jason had gone to bed, she'd found her grandfather in the kitchen microwaving a bag of milk chocolate chips with a bit of milk. Once he'd achieved a smooth consistency, he'd disappeared into his room with the bowl and one of Carolyn's kindergarten-size paintbrushes. Marie hadn't asked, but she'd looked around. She didn't see Betty, but Marie was fairly certain the other woman hadn't left yet.

Admittedly, pregnancy hormones seemed to have given her mind a prurient bent, but she thoroughly suspected her seventy-some-year-old grandfather of indulging in a little flavorful body painting with Betty.

"And no, I'm not jealous," Marie assured herself. She would also, however, not be moving back to her grandfather's when the time came. He and Jason didn't need her. In fact, she'd probably only be in the way there now.

"So, I'll get an apartment. And a job," she added as she

thought it through. "I'll help Luke find a good day care and when the time comes, the baby can go there, too. It's time to get on with my life." The buzzer rang for the cookies as if signifying agreement.

Luke had chosen to work at home that day. He wasn't seeing clients and he'd spent the day connected on-line with his office through his lap-top computer. Smelling the cookies, he left his study and came into the kitchen. He snatched himself a handful of the last batch, juggling them from hand to hand as they were still hot, and leaned back against the countertop.

"So," he asked, "what's cookin', good lookin'?"

Marie rolled her eyes. "Oh, please," she said. Opening the refrigerator, she retrieved the milk and poured Luke a glass, handing him the cup before he'd even realized he wanted it.

"Thanks."

"You're welcome."

Luke downed three cookies and half the milk while Marie nibbled on one. He noticed she'd picked her glass up several times but hadn't managed to actually drink anything.

"They're good," he said.

She nodded recognition of the compliment.

"Okay, what's wrong?"

"Nothing."

Luke snatched another handful of cookies and downed the first one. "Right. Nothing. What's Jason done now? He's driven very well our last few outings. We only had one near miss with a mailbox, which is at least inanimate. His coach swam him in three events last meet. I thought he was doing well."

"Oh, he is, he is. Well. Absolutely."

"Uh-huh. Then it's Ray."

"Oh, Grandpa's doing well, too. Really well."

Luke was not about to let Marie off the hook. He'd gotten to know her in the past few weeks. Something was bothering her. "But?" he prodded.

"It's just that he's thinking about going home. Probably next week."

"Well, we knew he wouldn't stay here forever. He's got his own home, Marie. You're not still worried about him and Betty, are you?"

"You think I'm jealous, don't you? Well I'm not, not at all. In fact, I'm very happy for them. Everybody should have somebody."

"Yes, they should," Luke agreed, watching her carefully as she got more and more agitated. "So, what's the deal?"

"Jason will go with them," Marie blurted.

Luke nodded. "Yes. We can offer him a place here, but he'll no doubt choose his own dad."

That gave her pause. "You'd let him stay on here?"

Luke shrugged. "Not all of his music is terrible. He's good with Carolyn. But the big reason is, I really think Ray and Betty might be thinking about tying the knot, Marie. They might like a little privacy for at least a little while. But like I said, I don't see Jason agreeing to stay here."

That was it. Just what she'd been afraid of. Luke had no intention of marrying her. If he did, it would be strictly out of duty. Ray would want time alone with his bride, but Luke didn't. That said it all, didn't it?

Taking a deep breath, Marie informed him, "When they go I'm going to go too, Luke."

The simple declaration staggered him. "What?"

Marie swung around to stare blindly out the window over the sink. "I'll help you find a good day care place for Carolyn. I've got a couple of leads." Marie gestured helplessly to the house next door. "I've met some of the neighbors. They've talked about how they handle their child care issues."

Luke ground his teeth. Child care issues. Is that how she thought of their relationship? A child care issue?

"We'll get that taken care of. Then I'm going to find an apartment."

"No...you...are...not."

Marie bowed her head. "You don't have to worry. I'll be fine. Really. I've got some insurance money. Enough to see me through."

Perhaps he hadn't been clear enough. "No."

Marie turned to face him. Her smile was tremulous. "You're off the hook, Sir Lancelot. You don't have to make the ultimate sacrifice. You've gotten my life enough back on track for me that I can handle things from here on. Grandpa's on the mend. He's got Betty now, thanks to you. Jason's going to make it, too. He's swimming anchor on the 400 free B relay tonight, did he tell you?" Marie held up a curled hand and opened up the fingers signifying release. "You're free."

Luke stared at her, then wheeled around and marched back into his study. He shut the door very carefully, knowing if he hadn't exhibited such care he'd have slammed it hard enough to split it.

"Damn the woman." For a whisper there was a lot of vehemence in the brief imprecation. "*Damn* her," he reiterated as he paced the small confines of the study. "Does she think she can march in and out of my life as the mood suits her?" He picked up a pencil, snapped it in two and irritably tossed it into the trash. "Use me to patch the pieces of her messed-up life back together and then pick up and leave?"

Luke shook his head. "I don't think so. Oh no, I don't think so. She's staying right here." He pointed to a spot in the carpet just in front of him. "Right here, I say, if I have to truss her up like a common criminal, I swear I'll do it. Yes, I will."

He paced some more while his blood boiled and his thoughts simmered. He could not believe this was happening. She'd agreed to the marriage, hadn't she? "Well, I'm

holding her to it. Get a damn bloodsucking lawyer if I have
to. See how much is left of her precious insurance money
then, by God. But she's honoring her commitment. Breach
of promise, that's what it is. A damn breach of promise."
It felt good to swear. It had been a while. "For her," her
muttered. "Gave up swearing for her. *She* decided it wasn't
good for Carolyn to hear and like a damn sheep to the
slaughter I went along. Well I'm swearing now, Madame
Prim Lips. Come listen to me now. Damn, damn, *damn!*"
And he threw in a *"hell!"* for good measure.

Luke sat on the corner of his desk, picked up the mug
of pencils and began using them like darts. His target was
the picture of Marie rocking Carolyn in his grandmother's
old rocking chair while they read together. Marie didn't
even know he'd had the shot enlarged and framed. Whenever she came in the room, the picture was safely hidden
behind the open door. Luke did not like wearing his heart
out on his sleeve for everyone to see.

"Bull's-eye!" A pencil hit Marie in the center of her
chest, right where she'd done the most damage to him.
"Chew my heart up into little pieces and spit it out, will
she?" He aimed another pencil dart and let it fly. "Well,
we'll just see about that."

Ammunition gone, Luke went to the window and heaved
it up. Leaning out he took deep, hopefully calming breaths
of the early fall, mildly crisp air. "Just exactly who barged
into whose life I'd like to know," he growled out the window. "It wasn't me hitting her, now was it? Oh, no. As I
recall, it was Marie and her idiot uncle who plowed into
me. An accident from which the new paint has barely dried
on my pride and joy, let me just point out. Barely dry and
she's already set to waltz out the door. Well, I'll be teaching her a new dance step or two, let me just tell you."

Luke suddenly realized he was ranting and raving at a
totally unimpressed maple tree. He glanced from side to
side and was relieved to note there were no neighbors out.

"The hell with this," he muttered in a much lower voice as he swiveled away from the window and threw himself into his desk chair. "The hell with this!"

For the rest of the afternoon he barked into the phone, sent curtly worded E-mails and generally made a hash of his reputation at the office for being calm and always on an even keel, no matter what the problem. "I'll give her until after the swim meet," he finally decided. "Then we'll have this out. "Whatever circuit in her brain has fried itself out will hopefully have rerouted itself by then. She's an intelligent woman. She'll see the right in this arrangement." Of course she would. "She needs me, damn it!"

After a frustrating afternoon where little was accomplished on either of the two main protagonists's parts, they ate dinner. Spaghetti. Ray, Betty and Carolyn raved over Marie's homemade French bread. The meal could have been cardboard for all the interest Luke or Marie showed. Finally they headed for the swim meet.

It was a nail biter. Even if it hadn't been close, Luke was a man. He would have kept score. He made marks after each event on his program that Marie couldn't decipher. She had to content herself with anxious glances at the scoreboard as the numbers seesawed back and forth.

Luke jumped up from his bench in the bleachered balcony. "For crying out loud, one handed touch. Automatic DQ. What's the ref looking at? He might want to check up on the swimmers in the pool every now and then. One of Northpoint's swimmers just made an illegal turn."

Marie pulled him down. "You're making a scene," she whispered. "I'm sure the referee knows his business."

"Yeah, yeah, whatever. Would you look at that? What's that supposed to be? It sure as heck isn't butterfly."

Marie glanced around. "Luke, hush. That child's parents are around here someplace, maybe right next to us. You'll hurt their feelings."

Luke grunted. "Yeah? Maybe they ought to teach their kid how to swim, then they won't get their feelings hurt."

"You're being impossible."

Luke shook his head. "Not me, babe. I'm not the one specializing in being impossible around here. I'm afraid you get to wear that crown all by yourself."

Impossible, her? "What?"

"Man, you'd think they have one decent breaststroker in this community. Is that asking so much? One decent breaststroker out of a town this size?" Luke made more tally points on his score sheet. "Why, I ought to go down there and show them how it's done."

Marie grabbed his arm, just in case. "You may get the opportunity," she muttered. "I think there are several people up here in the stands who are probably seriously thinking about throwing you in the water." Marie glanced anxiously at the scoreboard as the second to last race was posted. "We're down again."

Luke did some fast mental arithmetic. "Either the A relay has to take first or we've got to get both second and third here. Only the top three finishers score. It's not like an individual race. There are more points involved, too."

Marie gulped. "Oh, God. Let's hope the A relay takes it. Jason's swimming anchor on the B relay. He's not ready for this kind of pressure. You told me swimming was a team sport. You said it was never the bottom of the ninth, bases loaded, two out and your kid up to bat. You said that's why this was a perfect sport for a kid. That and it was hard to get hurt."

Grimly Luke watched the first swimmers go in the water. They each did four laps. Northpoint's lead swimmer far outdistanced their own. By the time the third swimmers entered the pool, it was clear Saint Joe Valley was out of contention for first place.

"Looks like I lied," Luke informed her and had Marie biting her nails for the first time in years. "I think it's officially the bottom of the ninth. Bases are loaded, there are two outs and our kid is coming up to bat.'' He nodded at the starting block Jason was mounting. Jason fiddled with his goggles and took a starting stance. Northpoint's A relay was just touching the finish pad. Saint Joe Valley's was half a pool length behind, steaming in. They would take second. Jason had to come through. The two B anchors entered the water together.

Marie closed her eyes. ''Oh, my God. I can't watch. I can't.''

Everyone in the stands rose to watch the final two swimmers. Ray, Betty and Luke screamed along with the crowd. Even Carolyn hopped up and down.

''Who is that?'' someone yelled.

''New kid. Jason somebody or other.''

''He any good?''

''Just okay.''

It was all Luke could do not to turn around and inform the old geezer to just watch. Jason would pull it off. ''Go, Jason,'' Luke yelled. ''You can do it!''

''Take him, son,'' Ray boomed out. ''Get him!''

Carolyn joined in, shrieking in her high voice, ''Go! Go! Go! Go!''

''Come on, kid, go!''

''He's doing it,'' Luke informed them all as if they couldn't see for themselves. ''He's pulling ahead.... Come on, Jason, strong turn, strong turn. Use the wall. That's it! Half a body length. He's got him by half a body length. Way to go, Jason. Keep it up.''

Marie looked around her, amazed. Didn't anybody realize the swimmers couldn't hear them? Their heads were underwater, for goodness' sake. But, heck, it was infectious. She began to yell, too. ''Swim faster, Jason! Swim faster!'' Jason flipped at the wall and began his third lap, heading to the far end of the pool once more.

''He's losing it,'' Luke said. ''Getting tired. Breathing

every other stroke. Don't blow it now, Jason," he murmured as he watched the other swimmer slowly gain. "I think he ate a wave," he intoned almost solemnly as they watched Jason struggle.

"He what?" Marie asked, horrified as Jason took the last turn almost neck and neck with his opponent.

"Swallowed some water," Luke clarified. "And I think the count is full now. Two strikes and three balls. *Come on,* Jason!"

Jason must have heard. He reached deep inside into some hidden reserve he probably didn't even know he had and refused to let the other swimmer take the lead. The touch pad times gave Jason the victory by a tenth of a second. The stands went nuts. The girl swimmers went nuts, surrounding Jason as he hauled himself out of the pool, hugging and kissing him. Jason's personal cheering section collapsed back into their seats with a collective sigh of relief.

"Did you see that?" Ray asked. "*Did you see that?* He did it! Jason did it!"

"Unbelievable" was all Luke could come up with in his exhausted state. "They won. Totally unbelievable. They win by two points and Jason's a hero."

Marie's grin couldn't get much wider and she cried while she smiled. Throwing herself against Luke's chest, she put her arms around his neck and about strangled him. "This is so cool," she sobbed. "So unbelievably cool. I'm so happy for him."

Luke patted her awkwardly on the back. He would never understand women. If she was all that happy, why was she crying? And couldn't she take a look around her and see that while this wasn't a family in the traditional sense, they all belonged together as a unit? Surely she couldn't be so stupid as to throw this away, could she?

They waited for Jason outside the locker room, Luke and Ray congratulating each other as though the victory had been theirs.

And in a way it had been, Marie decided. Her grandfather had given him life, set him out on the path. Jason had been in danger of stumbling for a while there, but Luke had steadied him, redirected him. Marie no longer had a shadow of a doubt. Jason would be okay.

"And here he is now, our resident hero, Jason Fort!"

Jason's grin split his face. "Did you see that, Dad? Did you see that, Marie, Luke? Did you catch all the girls kissing me at the end? Man, Marie, I'm telling you, I could live on those few minutes for the rest of my life." He scooped up Carolyn into his arms and nuzzled her neck. "How'd you like that, Caro? Want your Uncle Jase to teach you how to swim? What do you think, kiddo?" Carolyn just giggled.

Marie stood there like a proud mother and wondered how she could let Luke and Carolyn out of her life. But she was going to. It was only fair.

Ray offered to take them all to the Dairy Queen, but Jason was going out to celebrate "with the guys." One of the swimmer's parents owned a different fast-food franchise and had offered to treat. Marie was about to protest, but Luke stopped her with a look.

"This is how it should be," he whispered. "Let it go." So she did.

He'd been pleased, but four hours later he was ready to commit mayhem, murder, whatever it took to get her attention.

"She's avoiding me," he told Ray from a position at the end of Ray's bed after he'd invaded the older man's room. "She won't even talk about it."

Ray lowered his book and raised his eyebrows as he stared at Luke over the top of his half-moon reading glasses. "Talk about what?"

"She didn't tell you? Well, I'll tell you. Your stubborn granddaughter is all of a sudden out of the clear blue sky refusing to marry me. Says she's moving out into her own apartment when you and Jason leave next week.''

Ray closed his book and folded his hands over his chest. "Can't say I blame her.''

"Marie's lost all touch with reality, she's— What did you say?''

"Luke, women aren't like men,'' Ray explained kindly. "They don't think the same way we do.''

"No kidding. Now there's a revelation.''

"A woman needs to be romanced. Needs to know you want her enough to take the time to woo her.''

"That's bull.''

"No, that's gospel.''

Luke stuck his hands in his pockets and paced. At this rate, he was going to have to replace every carpet in the place. He'd have worn them out within the first year. Maybe they were under warranty. "Oh, I've noticed the way you've gone after my aunt Betty, don't think I haven't. I'm the one who picked up the copy of *Romeo and Juliet* for you when Marie didn't have time. I had to go out and buy vases for all the flowers you've bought Betty.''

"And it never occurred to you that Marie was hoping you'd get the hint when she asked you to do those things for me?''

Luke stopped his pacing long enough to glare in the direction of the bed. "Marie's too bright to fall for that tripe.''

Ray simply snorted his opinion of that.

"I'm serious.''

"So am I.''

"No, think about it. Marie's had one bad experience where she was married simply because my brother wanted her physically and marriage was the only way he could get her.''

"Damn straight.''

"I've already got one strike against me just being

Wade's brother. I'm trying to show her that with me she'd get stability. Reliability. Dependability.''

"Sounds like an advertisement for a damn mutual fund.''

"Ray, I'm being serious here.''

"That's the sad part.''

"I'm trying to give her what she needs, damn it all!'' Luke roared.

Ray roared right back. "She needs to know you care! Now listen up, I've got a recipe for chocolate body paint. She'll love it. You'll love it. All you have to do…''

Luke left the old man's bedroom convinced Ray was wrong. But he headed for the kitchen to see if the old geezer had used up all the chocolate chips the other night.

He ran smack-dab into Marie. She was sitting at the kitchen table, a mug of hot chocolate in front of her, her head in her hand. Luke came to a dead halt when he saw her.

"Hi,'' he said.

"Hi, yourself.''

"What's up?'' Luke asked and almost groaned as he felt a stirring in his groin.

"Not much. Can I get you something? Cup of tea? Instant coffee? Hot cocoa?''

Now was not the time to mention anything chocolate to him. He was already suffering and the mental images the word *chocolate* brought up at this point in time would increase his suffering greatly. This was all *her* fault. Marie, well, Jason with Marie right next to him, had barged into his life and now Luke was turning into a babbling idiot, fantasizing about painting a woman's body with a food confection. Better yet, having her paint his—never mind. The point was, she'd messed with his mind. The way he saw it, Marie owed him a few explanations. Ignoring Marie's question, Luke pulled out a chair, sat down and faced her.

"I want to know exactly what is going on in that pea-size little brain of yours."

Marie blinked. "Excuse me?"

"Not this time I won't. You're staying right here until we hash this out."

"Luke, have you been drinking?"

"No, but it's not a bad idea. Now your grandfather is trying to tell me that your walking out on our engagement, on Carolyn, on me is somehow my fault. I told him that was ridiculous but he insists that if I'd only get you flowers, take you up to a bedroom and pretend it was a desert island, paint your—" Luke gestured toward her chest "—with chocolate or some other foodstuff—" honey might not be a bad choice, he thought briefly "—you'd stay. I'm asking you point-blank. Will you stay if I do those things?"

Marie stared at her mug and blushed in embarrassment. "Would it be such a chore?"

He was nearly doubled over in pain just thinking about it. "I suppose I could," Luke said, appearing thoughtful, "if it was what you wanted."

Marie slapped the tabletop, making her spoon inside the mug jump. "Damn it, don't humor me. I refuse to be a charity project, some kind of service project, the last in a long line of socially responsible activities Luke Deforest bears on his broad shoulders."

Luke sat up straighter. "You think I have broad shoulders?"

"Oh, like you didn't know."

He put up a hand. "All right, all right, we'll come back to that."

"No, we won't."

Luke ignored her. "I don't understand women. I don't understand you. Where the hell is women's lib when you need it? Don't you get it?" Luke leaned intently forward. "Here, I'll spell it out for you. You and Wade got married because you had the hots for each other. You were both in a fever, right?''

It was true, but Luke would wait a hell of a long time before Marie would admit it out loud. He waited less than a minute.

"So, okay, the fire got out of control and you got burned." Luke sat back. "Didn't you learn anything from that?''

"I learned Wade and I were wrong for each other."

He gave her that much. "There is that, but now you need to extrapolate. Go from the particular to the general. Relationships based on sex don't work. I've watched Wade and guys just like him all my life. I know what I'm talking about.''

Marie looked at him more thoughtfully. "No, I don't think you do."

Luke blew out a frustrated breath and leaned forward again, punctuating his lecture with a finger jabbing the air. "You think I don't want some hot babe to single me out and come on to me for no other reason than just looking at me makes her sweat?''

Marie inhaled and took a chance. "Looking at you makes me sweat."

"Just thinking about you using chocolate body paint on me and then licking it off with nothing but your tongue has me so tied up in knots right now I don't think I could stand up and walk if the house was burning down and my life depended on it. You want to know why I came in here? I was going to see if there were any chocolate chips in the pantry. If Ray had used them up, I was going to check for ice-cream toppings. Butterscotch or carmel would probably work as well, don't you think?'' He shook his head to clear it. "That's how nuts, how depraved you've made me, Marie. You—what did you just say?''

"I said you make me sweat," Marie repeated quietly.

"I do?''

Solemnly, she nodded. They stared briefly at each other. Marie could *see* the longing in his eyes and hope flared. "Do I make you sweat?"

He could agree to that. "Well, yes. But whether I sweat or not is not the point." God, did she make him sweat. "I refuse to allow such an important decision as choosing the woman I will share the rest of my life with—and I intend for it to be the rest of my life—to be based on such an instinctual, primitive instinct. There's got to be more. Respect. Responsibility."

Marie added to the list. "Caring. Sharing."

"I care about you. All of you. Surely you could see how right we were together earlier tonight. And I want you to share your problems with me. I want to help."

"And I want to help you with your problems."

No man wanted to admit he needed help. Luke had been the rescuer for so long he didn't know if he could let himself be the rescuee, but if that's what it took... He nodded agreement. "You've helped a lot with Carolyn," he grudgingly admitted.

"Loving," Marie announced firmly, continuing the list he'd begun.

"Uh—"

"And sex, and I'm talking about love between a man and a woman who have all that other stuff on our list as a backdrop. Sex is an important, vital ingredient to loving."

Luke just stared at her.

Marie tried again. "Now it's your turn to get it. I'm agreeing with you, Luke. Sex can't stand on its own. But neither can duty and responsibility. One more time. I don't want to be your duty. I don't want to be your responsibility. Neither do I want to be your fixation."

"Exactly what do you want?"

He wanted her to spell it out, so she did as simply as she knew how. "To be your lover," Marie said, "with every nuance and possible shade of meaning the word has.

Luke, I love you. I don't want to leave next week but I will if I have to settle for second best.''

Luke reached across the table and took her hand. He made her sweat. She wanted him on all levels. It was just finally coming through. How much luckier could a man get? They could be each other's playthings *and* each other's caretakers. Both. At the same time. Amazing. But loving required wooing, so the other person knew she was desired. Suddenly all the silly gestures took on a new importance. ''Marie—''

''Hi, everybody, I'm home.''

Marie and Luke simultaneously groaned. ''Hi, Jason,'' they greeted as one.

Jason stopped, eyeing them suspiciously. ''What?''

Reluctantly, Luke released Marie's hand and stood. ''Nothing. Marie and I are getting married, that's all.''

Jason looked at Luke oddly. ''Like, I know. You already told me a long time ago. What can I say?'' he asked with a shrug. ''It's your funeral, man.'' But he said it with a grin.

''Yeah, and I intend to die happy.'' He snatched up a set of car keys from the countertop where he'd tossed them earlier. ''Marie, I'll be right back. Jason, congratulations once again. It's late. Better get up to bed. Gotta get up for early-morning practice, don't forget.''

''Coach canceled it on account of we won. All the guys were cheering me. Said we'd probably have had to do seven thousand yards if we'd lost.''

''That's great, Jason. Really great. Go to bed anyway. Marie, see if you can find those chocolate chips while I'm gone.''

''You gonna bake cookies, Marie?''

Marie smiled vaguely. ''Maybe. We'll see.'' Her nipples were already hardened in anticipation. She and Luke would have to see who cooked what.

"Good night, Jason," Luke said. "Marie, I'll be right back as soon as I pick up...the rest of the ingredients."

Marie went upstairs and bathed with a vanilla-scented soap. She didn't want the flavors to clash. When Luke slipped into her room he was laden with flowers. He didn't bother with vases, he simply strewed the flowers around the floor and on the bed, turning her room into a bower. She pulled the blanket and comforter down and spread a towel over the sheet. It was the last fastidious thought Marie had for a long time.

Much later, Luke propped himself up on an elbow and watched Marie's nipple pucker into a tight bud as he teased it with a long-stemmed carnation. They hadn't made love— they'd decided some things were best saved for the wedding night. "So," he demanded, "are you gonna marry me or what?"

"I'm not sure. Maybe you should try to convince me some more."

He growled and Marie threw her arms around him. "I love you, you crazy man. Yes, yes, yes."

Luke knew he could get away without saying the words. Marie wouldn't demand them. She'd figure being a male, he just wasn't in touch with himself or some such garbage. Action spoke louder than words, etc., etc. Well, she deserved them and she was going to get them. "Marie, I love you. I think I have for a long time. I think it's why I didn't visit much when you were married to Wade. I was jealous. And afraid to admit my feelings even to myself. It would mean I was no longer in control of myself. No longer captain of my ship because such an essential part of me was no longer my own."

Marie looped her hands around his neck. "What part?"

"My heart," Luke said simply and kissed her. "My heart." He kissed her again, deep and hard. Finally, he came up for air. "Any more butterscotch sauce left in that jar?" he asked.

* * * * *

Look Who's Celebrating Our 20th Anniversary:

Celebrate 20 YEARS

"Happy 20th birthday, Silhouette. You made the writing dream of hundreds of women a reality. You enabled us to give [women] the stories [they] wanted to read and helped us teach [them] about the power of love."

—*New York Times* bestselling author
Debbie Macomber

"I wish you continued success, Silhouette Books.... Thank you for giving me a chance to do what I love best in all the world."

—International bestselling author
Diana Palmer

"A visit to Silhouette is a guaranteed happy ending, a chance to touch magic for a little while.... It refreshes and revitalizes and makes us feel better.... I hope Silhouette goes on forever."

—Award-winning bestselling author
Marie Ferrarella

Silhouette ROMANCE™

Visit us at www.romance.net

PS20SRAQ1

Silhouette Romance is
proud to announce the
exciting continuation of

*This time, Thorton royal
family secrets are exposed!*

A Royal Masquerade
by Arlene James (#1432)
On sale March 2000

A Royal Marriage
by Cara Colter (#1440)
On sale April 2000

A Royal Mission
by Elizabeth August (#1446)
On sale May 2000

Available at your favorite retail outlet.

Where love comes alive™

Soldiers of Fortune...prisoners of love.

Back by popular demand, international bestselling author **Diana Palmer's** *daring and dynamic* Soldiers of Fortune *return!*

Don't miss these unforgettable romantic classics in our wonderful 3-in-1 keepsake collection. Available in April 2000.*

And look for a **brand-new** *Soldiers of Fortune* tale in May. Silhouette Romance presents the next book in this riveting series:

MERCENARY'S WOMAN

(SR #1444)

She was in danger and he fought to protect her. But sweet-natured Sally Johnson dreamed of spending forever in Ebenezer Scott's powerful embrace. Would she walk down the aisle as this tender mercenary's bride?

Then in January 2001, look for THE WINTER SOLDIER in Silhouette Desire!

Available at your favorite retail outlet.
*Also available on audio from Brilliance.